THE ROYAL HOUSE OF KAREDES

Many years ago there were two islands ruled as one kingdom—Adamas. But bitter family feuds and rivalry caused the kingdom to be ripped in two. The islands were ruled separately, as Aristo and Calista, and the infamous Stefani coronation diamond was split as a symbol of the feud, and placed in the two new crowns.

But when the king divided the islands between his son and daughter, he left them with these words:

"You will rule each island for the good of the people and bring out the best in your kingdom. But my wish is that eventually these two jewels, like the islands, will be reunited. Aristo and Calista are more successful, more beautiful and more powerful as one nation—Adamas."

Now King Aegeus Karedes of Aristo is dead, and the island's coronation diamond is missing! The Aristans will stop at nothing to get it back, but the ruthless sheikh king of Calista is hot on their heels.

Whether by seduction, blackmail or marriage, the jewel must be found. As the stories unfold, secrets and sins from the past are revealed and desire, love and passion war with royal duty. But who will discover in time that it is innocence of body and purity of heart that can unite the islands of Adamas once again?

All about the author...

MELANIE MILBURNE read her first Harlequin® novel when she was seventeen and has never looked back. She decided she would settle for nothing less than a tall, dark and handsome hero as her future husband. Well, she's not only still reading romance but writing it, as well! And the tall, dark and handsome hero? She fell in love with him on the second date and was secretly engaged to him within six weeks.

Two sons later, they arrived in Hobart, Tasmania—the jewel in the Australian crown. Once their boys were safely in school, Melanie went back to university and received her bachelor's and master's degrees.

As part of her final assessment she conducted a tutorial on the romance genre. As she was reading a paragraph from the novel of a prominent Harlequin® author, the door suddenly burst open. The husband she thought was working was actually standing there dressed in a tuxedo, his dark brown eyes centered on her startled blue ones. He strode purposefully across the room, hauled Melanie into his arms and kissed her deeply and passionately before setting her back down and leaving without a single word. The lecturer gave Melanie a high distinction and her fellow students gave her jealous glares! And so her pilgrimage into romance writing was set!

Melanie also enjoys long-distance running and is a nationally ranked top-ten swimmer in Australia. She learned to swim as an adult, so for anyone out there who thinks they can't do something—you can! Her motto is "Don't say I can't; say I CAN TRY."

Melanie Milburne

THE FUTURE KING'S LOVE-CHILD

THE ROYAL HOUSE
of
KAREDES

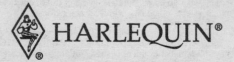

HARLEQUIN®

TORONTO • NEW YORK • LONDON
AMSTERDAM • PARIS • SYDNEY • HAMBURG
STOCKHOLM • ATHENS • TOKYO • MILAN • MADRID
PRAGUE • WARSAW • BUDAPEST • AUCKLAND

Dedicated to my beautiful daughter-in-law Dunya, who is one of the most courageous and loving young women I know. We are so delighted to have you as part of the family, it seems like you have been tailor-made just for us. Love you round the world and back. xxx

Recycling programs for this product may not exist in your area.

ISBN-13: 978-0-373-12875-4

THE FUTURE KING'S LOVE-CHILD

First North American Publication 2009.

Copyright © 2009 by Harlequin Books S.A.

Special thanks and acknowledgment are given to Melanie Milburne for her contribution to *The Royal House of Karedes* series

www.eHarlequin.com

Printed in U.S.A.

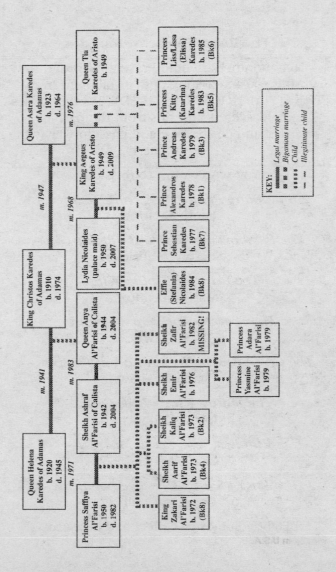

Queen Helena Karedes of Adamas
b. 1920
d. 1945

King Christos Karedes of Adamas
b. 1910
d. 1974

Queen Astra Karedes of Adamas
b. 1923
d. 1964

Queen Tia Karedes of Aristo
b. 1949

King Aegeus Karedes of Aristo
b. 1949
d. 2009

Lydia Nicolaides (palace maid)
b. 1950
d. 2007

Queen Anya Al'Farisi of Callista
b. 1944
d. 2004

Sheikh Ashraf Al'Farisi of Callista
b. 1942
d. 2004

Princess Saffiya Al'Farisi
b. 1950
d. 1982

Princess Liss/Lissa (Elissa) Karedes
b. 1985
(Bk6)

Princess Kitty (Katarina) Karedes
b. 1983
(Bk5)

Prince Andreas Karedes
b. 1979
(Bk3)

Prince Alexandros Karedes
b. 1978
(Bk1)

Prince Sebastian Karedes
b. 1977
(Bk7)

Effie (Stefania) Nicolaides
b. 1984
(Bk8)

Sheikh Zafir Al'Farisi
b. 1982
MISSING!

Sheikh Emir Al'Farisi
b. 1976
(Bk2)

Sheikh Kaliq Al'Farisi
b. 1973
(Bk2)

Sheikh Aarif Al'Farisi
b. 1973
(Bk4)

King Zakari Al'Farisi
b. 1972
(Bk8)

Princess Yasmine Al'Farisi
b. 1979

Princess Adara Al'Farisi
b. 1979

m. 1941   m. 1947   m. 1976
m. 1971   m. 1983   m. 1968

KEY:
Legal marriage
Bigamous marriage
Child
Illegitimate child

The Royal House of Karedes

Each month, Harlequin Presents is proud to
bring you an exciting new installment from
THE ROYAL HOUSE OF KAREDES. As the stories
unfold, secrets and sins from the past are
revealed and desire, love and passion war with
royal duty!

You won't want to miss out!

Eight volumes to collect and treasure!

Cassie marvelled at how he could inject so much into saying

CHAPTER ONE

CASSIE was just congratulating herself on getting through two hours of successfully shielding herself behind the Aristo palace's pillars and pot plants, dodging both the press and Prince Regent Sebastian Karedes, when she suddenly came face to face with him.

She swallowed thickly, her heart coming to a clunking stop in her chest as her eyes went to his inscrutable dark brown ones so far above hers. She opened her mouth to speak but her throat was too tight to get a single word out. She felt the slow creep of colour staining her cheeks, and wondered if he had any idea of how much over the last six years she had dreaded this moment.

'Cassie.' His deep voice was like a warm velvet glove stroking along the bare skin of her shivering arms. 'Have you only just arrived? I have not seen you until a few moments ago.'

Cassie moistened her dry-as-parchment lips with the tip of her tongue. 'Um….no,' she said, shifting her gaze sideways. 'I've been here all evening…'

A small silence began to weight the atmosphere, like humidity just before a storm.

'I see.'

Cassie marvelled at how he could inject so much into saying so little. Those two little words contained disdain and distrust, and something else she couldn't quite put her finger on.

'So why are you here?' he asked, his eyes narrowing even further. 'I do not recall seeing your name on the official guest list.'

Cassie swept the point of her tongue across her lips again, trying to keep her gaze averted. 'As part of my…um…parole programme, I took a job at the orphanage,' she said, loathing the shame she could feel staining her face. 'I've been working there for the last eleven months.'

When he didn't respond immediately Cassie felt compelled to bring her gaze back to his, but then wished she hadn't.

A corner of his mouth was lifted in an unmistakably mocking manner. '*You* are looking after children?'

She felt herself bristling. 'Yes,' she clipped out. 'I enjoy every minute of it. I'm here tonight with some of the other carers and educational staff. They insisted I attend.'

Another tight silence began to shred at Cassie's nerves. She would have given just about anything to have avoided coming here this evening. She had felt as if she had been playing a high stakes game of hide and seek all night, the strain of keeping out of the line of Sebastian's deep brown gaze had made her head pound with sickening tension. Even now the hammer blows behind her eyes were making it harder and harder for her to keep her manner cool and unaffected before him. His commanding and totally charismatic presence both drew her and terrified her, but the very last thing she wanted was for him to realise it.

She surreptitiously fondled the smooth pearls of the bracelet around her wrist, the only thing she still had left of her mother's, hoping it would give her the courage and fortitude to get through the next few minutes until she could make good her escape.

'Well, then,' he said as his eyes continued to skewer hers, that sardonic half-smile still in place. 'As the royal patron of the orphanage you now work for, I would have thought you would have made every effort to include yourself in this evening's proceedings rather than hide behind the flower arrangements.'

Cassie's chin came up. 'And have the press hound me for an exclusive photo and interview?' she asked. 'Not until my parole is up. Maybe then I'll think about it.'

His eyes began to burn with brooding intensity. 'I must say I am surprised you haven't already sold your story to the press, Cassie,' he said. 'But perhaps I should warn you before you think about doing so. One word about our...' he paused over the word for an infinitesimal moment '...past involvement, and I will have you thrown back into prison where the majority of the population of Aristo believes you still belong. Have I made myself clear?'

Cassie felt anger run through her like a red-hot tide. 'Perfectly,' she bit out, her eyes flashing with fury. How she hated him at that moment. The injustice she had suffered was bad enough, but to have him threaten her in such a ruthless manner was abominable. But until her parole was up what else could she do but pretend she had nothing to hide? She had learned the hard way that silence was her best defence—her *only* defence.

Sebastian was conscious of the time and the press of the crowd behind them. He had told his bodyguards to give him a few minutes but he knew they would come looking for him soon. His formal duties for the evening were more or less over and the crowd would soon begin to disperse. But he hadn't seen Cassandra Kyriakis for close to six years, and he had to make sure she was not going to be a threat to his future as King of Aristo now she was out of prison. They had parted on such bitter terms; he had been so blisteringly angry at the way she had ended their affair, and her betrayal still rankled even after all this time.

When he had caught sight of her disappearing behind one of the pillars he had thought he must have conjured up her image, so great was the shock and effect on him of seeing her again. It had taken every bit of the thirty-two years of his royal training to keep his reaction hidden. He had formally opened the gala, chatted with the official guests, smiled in all the right places, but all the while wondering how he could capture five minutes in private with her.

But now that he had, he wondered if it had been wise to seek her out. Every pore of his skin was erect with awareness, his nostrils automatically flaring in the primal hunt for her feminine scent, and his groin tightening with an ache so intense he had trouble standing still.

It annoyed him to find his body still hummed with desire for her. He had considered himself over her, and yet one glimpse into that emerald gaze of hers had made him realise there was still a place deep inside him that responded almost involuntarily when he looked at her. It was as if she had secretly planted a tiny fish hook in his chest all those years ago, and every time their eyes met he felt its tiny but still-painful tug.

For all her supermodel beauty there was no escaping the fact she was a sleep-around socialite tart who had wantonly led him on only to dump him, no doubt for the glory of having bedded a prince. He had met plenty of women like her before and since, but he had not seen her rejection and betrayal coming and that irked him more than he wanted to admit. No one had done that to him before. He had never had his pride rubbed in the dust like that, but then that was Cassie for you. She had come along with those amazing green eyes, her long, silky, blonde hair and sensually seductive wiles, and snatched the breath right out of his chest.

His eyes ran over her appraisingly. She was wearing a shell-pink sheath of a dress that clung lovingly to her willowy frame, highlighting the small but perfect globes of her breasts, skimming over the slight, almost boyish hips and the endless legs that had so many times wrapped around his in the throes of their heated passion. Her slender arms were bare, but on her left wrist she wore a pearl bracelet which he had noticed her fiddling with earlier with those slim fingers of hers.

Sebastian had to remind himself Cassandra Kyriakis had killed her father with those very delicate feminine hands. The lesser charge of manslaughter didn't make her any less of a murderess, or at least certainly not according to the press and public's view. But right now she didn't look capable of doing anyone harm. She looked nervous, agitated almost, her bottom lip being savaged by her small white teeth, and her body looked tense and ill at ease.

A little stab of guilt pierced him. His threat had perhaps been a little heavy-handed and ruthless, but he had to be absolutely sure she would keep quiet about their previous relationship. He would make it worth her while, although any dealings he had with her now would have to be conducted under the strictest secrecy. The press were like sniffer dogs when it came to the Karedes royal family and it would be risky even being seen talking to her, but it would be well and truly worth it if he could achieve what he wanted. He knew it just by looking at her. The old adage might have it that revenge was a dish best served cold, but the sort of revenge Sebastian had in mind was going to be hot—blazingly so, for he had a score to settle with her and he knew where it would be settled best.

In his bed.

A palace official approached, and Sebastian exchanged a few words with him, turning back barely thirty seconds later to find Cassie had completely disappeared. He narrowed his gaze and scanned the crowd, looking for a flash of baby-pink chiffon or platinum-blonde hair, but there was none.

'Are you looking for someone in particular, Your Royal Highness?' the junior official asked. 'I can organise security to find them for you if you like.'

Sebastian schooled his features into impassivity. There was only one aide in the palace he could trust with this sort of minefield situation, and this unfortunately was not him. 'No,' he said curtly. 'That will not be necessary.'

The young man gave an obsequious bow and moved away. It was only then that Sebastian saw the tiny bracelet lying on the floor where Cassie had been standing such a short time ago. He bent down and picked it up, his fingers absently stroking over the string of smooth orbs as he scanned the dispersing crowd once more.

As yet another official approached, Sebastian surreptitiously slipped the bracelet into his trouser pocket, inwardly smiling as he let the pearls slide through his fingers, one by one.

Cinderella might have escaped from the ball, but this particular Prince Charming was going to lure her back to him with something even more fitting than a glass slipper.

'Cassie, what's wrong?' Angelica, Cassie's flatmate, asked as soon as she came in. 'You look totally flustered. Is everything all right?'

Cassie closed the door and leaning back against it, pinched the bridge of her nose with two fingers, her eyes squeezed tightly shut in a vain effort to ease the tension about to explode behind her temples. 'No…no, I'm fine, just a headache.' She opened her eyes and, pushing herself away from the door, moved farther into the flat.

'Is Sam OK?'

'Of course he is,' Angelica assured her. 'He was a bit unsettled at first, but I promised him you would be back as soon as you could, and he eventually went to sleep and hasn't stirred since. I just checked him a few moments ago. He's out for the count.'

'That's good,' Cassie said, expelling a tiny breath of relief, although her stomach was still full of fist-like knots.

'You worry too much, Cassie,' Angelica admonished her gently. 'Sam's five years old now. He needs to learn to be away from you occasionally. You can't keep him tied to you for ever, you know.'

'I know. It's just he's never really got over being separated from me when I was in prison,' Cassie said, trying not to think of that harrowing time when Sam's desperate cries had echoed in her head for months after he was wrenched from her arms. She had been allowed to give birth to him inside the high walls of the Aristo prison and keep him with her until he turned three. Of all the suffering she had endured over the years that had been by far the very worst. Relinquishing Sam had felt like having one of her limbs torn off. She still had nightmares about it, waking up in a lather of sweat, in case someone had crept into the flat during the night and stolen her baby son away from her all over again.

'You're the one who hasn't got over it,' Angelica said astutely. 'Put it in the past where it belongs. You're on a roll now, Cassie. Your work at the orphanage is your ticket to a new life off the island once your parole is up. And, speaking of the orphanage, how did the fund-raising event go at the palace? Did you see Prince Sebastian? Is he as handsome as he looks in all the press photos?'

'Um…yes, he is…' Cassie felt her heart give a painful squeeze as she thought of that brooding, dark, all-seeing gaze. She had taken a huge risk leaving the gala so abruptly, but she couldn't have coped with another torturous minute in

Sebastian's company. The air between them had been charged with sexual energy; she had felt it as soon as she looked into his face. She had felt the slow burn of his gaze through the fine layers of her dress, as if he was recalling every intimate inch of her and how he had pleasured her in the past. A shiver travelled the entire length of her spine at the thought of how she had come apart time and time again in his arms. Had he guessed she still felt the same way? *Oh, please, God, don't let him have guessed!*

Her fingers automatically went to her left wrist, her heart giving a sudden lurch of panic when she found it totally bare. 'Oh, no!'

'What's wrong?' Angelica asked. 'You've gone as white as a ghost.'

Cassie swung around and backtracked her way to the front door of the tiny flat with agitated steps. 'I've lost my bracelet,' she said, searching the floor in rising desperation. 'My mother's pearl one. It must have fallen off on the way home. I was sure it was still on my wrist when I was at the palace.'

'Maybe it fell off in the cab,' Angelica suggested. 'You could call up the company and ask them to look for it.'

Cassie turned to look at her friend. 'I didn't take a cab home.'

Angelica's eyes widened. 'You walked home in the dark in *those* shoes?'

No, I ran home in the dark, Cassie felt tempted to confess but instead said, 'I felt like I needed the fresh air. The palace was crowded and…and stuffy.'

'I'll get a torch for you,' Angelica said. 'I'll mind Sam while you retrace your steps, or do you think we should wait until morning when we can both search?'

Cassie shook her head determinedly. 'No, someone might pick it up before then. I'll go a few blocks and see if I can find it. I'm sure it can't be too far away.'

'Make sure you take your mobile with you,' Angelica said. 'You don't know who might be out on the streets at this time of night. And you had better get changed. You are going to stick out like a sore thumb in that dress.'

Cassie quickly checked on Sam on her way to her room to change into a track suit and sneakers. He was sleeping peacefully, his beautiful face so like his father's it made her heart contract again in unbearable pain. Her little son would never be able to run to his daddy and place his arms around his neck; he would never be able to look him in the those deep brown eyes exactly the same shade as his for reassurance, or for the guidance and support she could already see he so desperately needed.

He had been cheated of so much, just as she had, but she was going to do her utmost to make it up to him. As soon as her parole period was up she and Sam would be off the island and begin a new life, a life where no one knew who Cassie was, what she had supposedly done and—even more importantly—whose child she had secretly borne.

CHAPTER TWO

THE cobbled streets were lit with the occasional lamp post but even so Cassie felt the menacing shadows of the night creeping towards her with every step she took. She shone the narrow beam of the torch Angelica had given her around, but so far she had found nothing but the occasional cigarette butt or gum wrapper. It made her think of her father, how he as the town mayor had orchestrated a campaign to clean up the ancient streets of Aristo, even though his own home had contained the most filthy of all secrets.

Cassie gave a little shudder and forced the memories back and continued on her mission, her head down, her steps carefully measured as she went as close to the palace as she dared.

She was no more than three blocks away when she suddenly came up short, her heart thudding in fear as a pair of large male sports shoes were illuminated by her torch. She brought the beam shakily upwards to find Sebastian Karedes, dressed similarly to her in a dark track suit, his eyes unreadable as they meshed with hers.

'Looking for something, Cassie?' he asked.

Cassie had never imagined there would be a time in her life when she would have rather met a mugger on a dark street than the man she had once loved with all her being. She had faced fear before, many times, gut-wrenching fear that most people thankfully never had to face. But this was something else again. Sebastian had the power to destroy her in a way even her father hadn't been able to do. Everything she had fought so long and hard for seemed to be hinged on these next few moments. The tension built in her spine; she could feel it moving up vertebra by vertebra, a vicelike grip that made her stomach crawl with the long spidery legs of apprehension.

'I…I seem to have lost my bracelet,' she said, lowering the torch. 'I thought if I retraced my steps I might find it.'

'You left without saying goodbye,' he said. 'I was hoping for a few more minutes with you in private. There are some things I would like to discuss with you.'

Cassie turned off the torch with her thumb in case the soft light showed the fear on her face. 'I'm not sure it's such a good idea for us to be seen anywhere together, Sebastian,' she said. 'You know what the paparazzi are like. You are about to be crowned as King. It would not do your reputation any favours being seen talking with an ex-prisoner.'

'There is no one about now,' he said. 'We could go back to your place. We would not be disturbed there, I am sure.'

Cassie was glad he couldn't see the way her eyes suddenly flared in panic. Sam was not the deepest of sleepers. He still occasionally wet the bed, which made him wake up distressed and call out for her. 'No,' she said, far too quickly. 'I mean… it's awkward…I…I have a flatmate.'

'A man?'

'No.'

'You have no present lover?'

Cassie felt the fine hairs on the back of her neck start to prickle at the seemingly casually asked question. Unless she turned the torch back on she had no way of reading his expression, and even then there was no guarantee she would be able to decipher what motive lay behind his query. Sebastian was a master of disguising his feelings, if indeed he had any. She had often wondered if his aloofness and slight air of condescension were a guise or an innate part of his personality. She had never quite made up her mind either way. He had been trained from a young age to step up to the throne upon the death of his father, which had occurred only a few months ago. That he was prepared to risk being seen with her was as surprising as it was deeply disturbing.

Cassie knew she was at risk of revealing too much. She could feel it now even under the cloak of darkness. The pulse of her blood was like thunder in her veins, her breasts felt tight and sensitive, and that secret feminine place he had possessed so many times throbbed with a hollow ache that was almost painful.

'I've been seeing someone,' she lied, hoping it would put an end to the undercurrent of attraction she could feel coming towards her.

'The same person you were seeing when you ended our affair?' he asked with bitterness sharpening his tone.

'No...someone else.' *Oh, how easily the second lie followed the first,* she thought.

'How serious is your relationship with this man?' he asked.

'Serious enough.'

'Serious enough to risk your freedom?'

Cassie dropped the torch, but even as she heard it clatter its way over the cobblestones she was unable to move. 'W-what are you suggesting?' she asked in a dry croak.

He bent down and retrieved the torch and, flicking it on, shone it on her face. 'How about we go back to my private quarters and discuss it?' he said.

Cassie blinked against the probe of the torch's beam. 'I am not sure there is anything we have to discuss,' she said, 'or at least nothing of interest to me.'

'On the contrary, I think it will be of the greatest interest to you,' he said, and turned off the torch with a click that sounded portentous in the still night air. 'You see, Cassie, I have something of yours.'

Yes, well, so do I, Cassie thought wryly, once again glad of the mantle of darkness so he couldn't read the apprehension on her face. 'My bracelet?' she asked hopefully. 'Do you have it with you?'

'No, it is at the palace.'

Cassie wondered if he was telling the truth, but she could hardly ask to search him. She gnawed at her lip for a moment. 'Could you have someone send it to me in the post?' she asked.

'Not unless you want to take the risk of it being mislaid or perhaps even stolen,' he said. 'I would prefer to hand it over to you face to face. It looks rather valuable.'

'It is,' Cassie said, her heart sinking as she realised she would have no choice but to accompany him back to the palace. They had met in secret so many times in the past, just the thought of doing so again conjured up so many intimate images. She wondered if Sebastian was revisiting any of them in his own mind.

'Come.' He placed a firm hand at her elbow. 'There is a back entrance to the palace a couple of blocks from here.'

Cassie reluctantly fell into step beside him, her flesh burning under the touch of his hand. They walked in silence, she because she didn't know what to say and he—she assumed—because he was waiting until he had her somewhere secluded to discuss whatever he had planned for her. That there was a plan she was in no doubt. Proud men like Sebastian Karedes did not take rejection on the chin, and her rejection of him had been particularly cruel.

Sebastian led her through a wrought-iron gate where an aide was waiting. They exchanged a brief exchange before the man led the way to a suite of rooms down a long, marbled corridor. The walls were lined with generations of the Karedes family; all their eyes seemed to be following Cassie as she walked soundlessly by Sebastian's side.

The aide opened a door leading into a private lounge. The furniture was modern and, although the palace was centuries old, somehow the mix of old and new worked brilliantly.

'So, Cassie,' Sebastian said once the aide had closed the door on his exit. 'This is like old times, is it not?'

Cassie searched his features for a moment but couldn't read his inscrutable expression. 'I'm not sure what you mean,' she hedged, although her mind had already taken a wild guess.

He reached out and lifted her chin with the blunt end of one of his long fingers. She felt a shiver of reaction cascade like a shower of exploding fireworks down her spine at that jolt of skin-to-skin electricity passing from his body to hers. It had always been this way between them. The air in the room was charged with the electric tension of sexual attraction. She could see it in the dark, brooding intensity of his gaze; she could sense it in the sensual curve of his mouth and, God help her, she could feel it in the core of her body where her intimate muscles were already starting to ache.

'You and I always met in secret, did we not?' he said, looking down at her mouth for a pulsing moment. 'I see no reason to change that now.'

Cassie stepped back out of his light but eminently disturbing hold, her legs almost tripping over themselves in her haste to put some distance between her body and his. 'You are surely not suggesting we resume our illicit affair?' she said in a brittle keep-away-from-me tone.

He gave a little shrug. 'We were good together, Caz,' he said, using the private nickname he had chosen for her all those years ago. 'You know we were.'

Cassie wanted to cover her ears and block out the sensual lure of his deep velvet-toned voice. God, did he have any idea of how he still affected her? How could he possibly think she had forgotten how good they had been together? The moment she had set eyes on him again it had been as if the faint background pulse in her body she had done her best to ignore had suddenly come to fervent life again. It was thumping now beneath her skin, so strong and heavy it made her feel dizzy.

She had been *so* strong for all this time. Now was not the time to fall apart. Not now when she was so close to final freedom. She had just a matter of weeks to go until her parole period was finished. Once that time was up she would leave Aristo with Sam, making a new life for them both. This was not the time to be drawn back into Sebastian Karedes's sensual orbit, no matter how very tempting it was.

Cassie pulled back her shoulders and sent him a glittering glare. 'You seem to be forgetting something, Sebastian. We ended our association six years ago.'

'You ended it, Cassandra. I did not,' he said with an unmistakably embittered edge to his voice.

Cassie lifted her chin even higher. 'I *can* still call you Sebastian, can't I, or would you prefer Your Royal Highness? Should I have bowed or curtsied when I ran into you on the street? How very remiss of me.'

Something moved at the side of his mouth as if her words had pulled on a tight string beneath the skin on his jaw. 'Sebastian will be fine,' he said through tight lips. 'At least while we are alone.'

This time it was Cassie's mouth that went tight. 'I do not intend being alone with you in future,' she said with a deliberately haughty look. 'Please give me back my bracelet. I need to get home.'

His eyes burned into hers. 'You are forgetting yourself,

Cassie,' he said. 'That is not the way to speak to a member of the royal household. I will dismiss you when I see fit, not the other way around.'

'What are you going to do about it, Sebastian?' she asked, throwing him another mocking glare. 'Lock me up in the palace tower and throw away the key? I'm sure I'll institutionalise rather quickly considering where I've spent the last few years, don't you agree?'

He held her gaze for an interminable pause but Cassie was determined not to look away first.

She could *do* this.

She could stand here and fire back at him without breaking down.

She *had* to do this.

His expression was nothing short of contemptuous as he held her look. 'Your anger towards me is rather misplaced, Cassie,' he said. 'You were the one to bring an end to our affair by flaunting a host of lovers in my face. If anyone has a right to be angry it should be me.'

Cassie gave herself a mental kick. He was right. She had told him a parcel of lies in an attempt to get away from the island, never dreaming it would backfire on her the way it had.

'Is that not correct, Cassie?' he prompted again with steely purpose.

She pressed her lips together and lowered her gaze from the searing probe of his. 'Yes…' she said. 'That is correct.'

'Is that who you are rushing off to return to now?' he asked. 'One of your many lovers? No doubt you are keen to make up for lost time, *ne?*'

Cassie now understood what it felt like to be hoist with one's own petard and it wasn't particularly comfortable. 'There is just the one person I care about now,' she answered.

There was a short but tense pause.

'Do you intend to marry this man?' he asked.

Cassie brought her eyes back to his. 'No, I do not.'

She saw the disdain in his gaze as it warred with hers, and, although he didn't say the words out loud, she could hear them ringing in the stiff silence.

Whore.

Slut.

Jailbird.

'I want to see you again,' Sebastian said with a masklike expression. 'Here, tomorrow, for lunch, and do not think about saying no.'

Cassie felt her eyes go wide and struggled to control her escalating panic. 'I-I'm working at the orphanage t-tomorrow,' she stammered. 'We're short staffed as it is. I can't just breeze out for lunch.'

His stance was implacable. It was clear in the months since his father had died Sebastian had become accustomed to having each and every one of his words obeyed. 'I will have my personal secretary notify the head of the orphanage that you have an official appointment at the palace.'

Cassie gave a tight swallow. 'What will the press make of that if they hear about it?' she asked.

'They will not hear about it from me,' he said. 'If on the other hand you get it in your pretty little blonde head to inform them yourself, I have already warned you what will happen if you do.'

She glared at him in fury. 'You think you can blackmail me, don't you?'

He gave her an imperious smile. 'If you want your bracelet back, then, yes, I am sure I can blackmail you to do whatever I want.'

Cassie clenched her hands into fists. 'You bastard,' she ground out bitterly.

'Careful, Cassie,' he warned her silkily. 'I don't think a charge of common assault will go down too well right now with your parole officer, will it?'

Right now Cassie felt as if it would be worth it just to slap that arrogant look off his too-handsome face. 'I am going to ask you one more time,' she said in a cold, hard tone. 'Give me back my bracelet.'

He held up his hands above his head. 'Come and get it,' he said, nodding towards his left-hand trouser pocket.

Cassie felt her heart skip a beat at the challenging glint in his dark eyes. She pulled in a breath, and with a hand that was nowhere near as steady as she would have liked, slipped it tentatively into his pocket. Her belly quivered as she felt the distinctive swell of his body against her searching fingers, but there was no bracelet. She pulled out her hand and sent him a fulminating look.

'Try the other one,' he said with an inscrutable smile. 'I must have forgotten which side I put it.'

Cassie sucked in another furious breath and a little less cautiously this time dug her hand into his right pocket, but before she could locate the circle of pearls his hands came down and held hers against his now pulsing full-on erection. Her eyes flew to his in shock, the erotic feel of him even through the layers of fabric making her heart race out of control.

'How much do you want your bracelet?' he asked, his eyes now almost black with diamond-hard purpose.

She felt him surging against the palm of her hand and her stomach turned over, every pore of her flesh crawling with a desire so overwhelming she was sure he could sense it. 'What exactly are you asking me to do, Sebastian?' she asked in a brittle tone. 'Get down on my knees and service you like the whore you think you can make me?'

His pupils flared, making his eyes even darker, like bottomless pools of ink. 'If anyone has made you a whore it is yourself,' he said. 'I know the game you are playing, Cassie. You deliberately left that bracelet behind this evening, did you not?'

Cassie threw him a withering look. 'That really would have been casting pearls before swine, now, wouldn't it?'

He pulled her hands away from his body, bracketing her wrists either side of her body in a movement so sudden she felt every last breath of air rush out of her chest. 'I must say I like this new hard-to-get game you are intent on playing,' he said, pressing his hardened lower body into the softness of hers. 'It makes me all the more determined to have you.'

Cassie's gaze went to his mouth, her stomach doing a quick flip-flop as she realised his intention. But instead of pulling out of his hold, she pressed herself closer as his mouth came down to hers.

It was an angry kiss, a kiss of built-up resentment and bitterness, but even so she couldn't stop herself from responding to it. His tongue didn't ask for permission to enter her mouth, it demanded it, thrusting between her trembling lips with an intention that was as deeply erotic as it was irresistible. His mouth ground against hers, drawing from her whimpers, not of protest but of pleasure. Her body moulded itself against his, seeking his hardness, thrilling in the feel of his arousal, her heart racing at the thought of the dangerous game they both were playing.

One of his hands slid beneath her track-suit top, his warm palm rediscovering the weight of her bra-less breast. Cassie's belly contracted when he took her nipple between his thumb and index finger, the gentle pinch and pull caress making her breathless with desire.

Her hands went on their own journey of rediscovery, pulling his T-shirt free so she could feel his skin beneath her palms. She felt the heavy thud of his heart against her hand, before she took her hand lower to feel the shape of him through his track pants. She heard him groan as she stroked his length, and she increased the speed and pressure of her caresses.

He lifted his mouth off hers to place it hot and moistly over her breast, sucking on her, not too hard, not too soft, but enough to have her senses spinning madly out of control.

He pulled her hand away from his body and looked down at her with his eyes blazing with desire. 'So it is the same for you as it is for me,' he said. 'Six years has done nothing to change the chemistry between us.'

Cassie wanted to deny it, but her hand was still tingling where she had touched him, so instead she said nothing.

He brought up her chin and pressed a brief hard kiss to her mouth. 'You can have your bracelet back tomorrow,' he said. 'I will give it to you after we have lunch together.'

'That's blackmail.'

Sebastian gave her a nonchalant smile. 'No,' he said. 'That is a promise.'

He watched as her mouth tightened. 'My bracelet is valuable to me, but not enough to lose my self-respect,' she said. 'If I sleep with you again it will be because I want to, not because I have been forced to.'

Sebastian held her fiery look for a moment. It was a sweet salve to his pride to know she still wanted him. He could take her here and now, he could see it in her eyes, the way they kept flicking to his mouth, her tongue sneaking out to her lips to taste where he had been. But he wanted to keep her dangling, just as she had done to him in the past.

'All right,' he said, moving away to the other side of the room where a desk was situated. He unlocked one of the drawers and, taking out her bracelet, came back to where she was standing.

He took her right hand and laid the pearls against the soft

bed of her palm, then gently closed her fingers over them, one by one. 'I think you should have the safety catch repaired before you wear it again,' he said, his eyes meshing with hers.

Cassie swallowed as his eyes burned into hers, their sensual promise heating her blood all over again.

'If you do not turn up tomorrow as arranged, Cassie, I will come to the orphanage and fetch you myself,' he said with a glint of steel in his gaze.

Cassie felt something small and dark scuttle inside her chest cavity. Would he do it? Would he draw such attention to himself or was he calling her bluff? How could she risk it either way? 'I-I will be here,' she said, slipping her eyes out of reach of his.

He touched her briefly on the curve of her cheek with the tip of one finger. 'See you tomorrow, Cassie,' he said, and reached for the bell to summon his aide. 'I am already looking forward to it.'

Within seconds Cassie was being driven home, her chest feeling as if a headstone had been placed inside it, making it hard to pull in a breath. She looked back at the glittering ancient palace as the dark car growled like a panther as it ate up the cobbled streets, and suppressed a little shiver.

Until tomorrow…

CHAPTER THREE

SAM'S little hand suddenly clutched at the front of Cassie's uniform, his eyes huge in his stricken face. 'You're c-coming back again, aren't you, Mummy?'

Cassie squatted down to his level and looked deep into his troubled gaze. 'Yes, sweetie, of course I am.'

His expression was still white with worry. 'You're not g-going to be locked away like before, are you?'

Cassie suppressed a frown as she hugged him close. She had always tried to be as honest with him as possible without distressing him with details too difficult for him to understand. After all, it seemed pointless pretending the fifteen-foot-high barbed wire and concrete enclosure of the Aristo prison was some sort of luxury accommodation, but she had never gone into the sordid details of why she had had to be housed there. But it made her wonder who had been talking to him about her past and why. He was only just five years old. Apart from her flatmate and close friend, Angelica, he was with her all the time at the orphanage. But it was clear someone had said something to him, or perhaps he had overheard some staff members talking.

'Baby, that was a long time ago and it's never going to happen again, I promise you with all my heart,' she said, holding him gently by his thin little shoulders. 'I am never going to be separated from you again. *Never.*'

Sam's chin wobbled slightly and his stammer continued in spite of his effort to control it. 'I heard Spiro t-talking to one of the carers,' he said. 'He said you k-killed my grandfather, and that you said it was an accident, but no one believed you.'

Cassie bit down on her bottom lip. She had naively hoped this conversation was several years away, but the gardener at the orphanage had never liked her since she had spurned his advances a few months ago. But that he would discuss her past with one of the children's carers was reprehensible to say the least. She loved her job. She *needed* her job. It wasn't just the money—the wage was hardly what anyone would call lucrative; it was the fact that for once in her life she was able to give something back to those in need. She had misspent her youth, wasted so many precious years being seen at the right parties with the right people, turning into a glamorous coat hanger for the 'right' clothes, mouthing the vacuous words that marked her as a shallow socialite looking for a good time.

The more her prestige-conscious and controlling father had protested, the more outrageous she had become. Cassie hadn't needed the prison psychologist to tell her why she had behaved the way she had. She had known it from the very first time she had realised what her birthday represented. It was certainly not a date to be celebrated, but she hadn't realised the sick irony of it until she had faced the judge and jury.

Cassandra Kyriakis had not just killed her father, but on the day she had come into the world she had taken her mother's life as well.

Cassie hugged Sam close to her chest, breathing in the small-child scent of him, her heart swelling with overwhelming love. 'We'll talk about this when I get back and Mummy will explain everything. I won't be away long, my precious,' she said. 'I'm just having a quick lunch with...with a friend.'

Sam eased back in her hold to look up at her. 'Who with, Mummy? Have I met them?' he asked.

Cassie shook her head and gently ruffled the black silk of his hair. 'No, you have never met him,' she said, her heart aching at the thought of her little boy never knowing his father. She had never known her mother and often wondered if her life would have been different for her if she had.

'He's a very important person on Aristo,' she added. 'He is soon to be the king.'

Sam's eyes were like wide black pools. 'Can I give you a picture to take for him to hang at his palace?' he said. 'Do you think he would like that?'

She smiled at him tenderly, her heart squeezing again. 'You know something, sweetie, I think he would.'

He scampered over to his little wooden desk and brought back a coloured drawing of a dog and a cat and something she thought looked like a horse. 'If he likes it I can do another one and you can give it to him the next time you see him,' he said with a shy smile.

'That's a great idea,' Cassie said and, folding the picture neatly, put it in her handbag. She didn't like to tell her little son she didn't intend seeing Sebastian again. Instead she got to her feet and, holding his hand, led him back to Sophie, one of the chief carers at the orphanage. She bent down and gave him another quick hug and kiss, and, while Sophie cleverly distracted him with a puzzle she had set out, Cassie quietly slipped out.

The palace was no less intimidating in the daylight than it had been the night before. With commanding views over most of the island, including the resort and Bay of Apollonia and the casino and the Port of Messaria, the royal residence was much more than a landmark. Every time Cassie had seen those twinkling lights from the prison on the western end of the island she had thought of the richness of Aristo as a kingdom and how Sebastian's father, King Aegeus, had built it up to be the wealthy paradise it was today.

It was only as Cassie came up to the imposing front gates that she realised Sebastian hadn't given her instructions on how to gain access. But she need not have worried, for waiting at the entrance was the aide, Stefanos, who had been present the previous evening. After a quick word to the guards on duty he led her through the palace, using a similar route to the night before, but this time taking her to a sitting room overlooking the formal gardens of the palace.

'The Prince Regent will be with you shortly,' Stefanos informed her and closed the door firmly on his exit.

Cassie let out her breath in a ragged stream and looked to where a small dining table with two chairs had been assembled in front of one of the large windows.

The door opened behind her and she turned to see Sebastian enter the room. He was wearing charcoal-grey trousers and a white open-necked shirt, the cuffs rolled back casually past his wrists. It didn't seem to matter what he wore, he still had an imposing air about him, an aura of authority and command that only added to his breathtakingly handsome features.

'I am glad you decided to come,' he said into the silence.

'I figured the orphanage is not quite ready for an impromptu visit from royalty,' Cassie said, thinking on her feet. 'The press attention might have upset the children.'

He frowned as he came closer. 'Seeing you at the gala last night was a shock,' he said, looking down at her. 'A big shock.'

'Did you think I had escaped from prison and had come to

gatecrash your party?' she asked, not quite able to subdue the bitterness in her tone.

He gave her a long and studied look. 'No, Cassie, I did not think that. It was just that I wish I had been told you had been released.'

'You could have made your own enquiries,' she pointed out and, with another embittered look, tacked on, 'discreetly, of course.'

A two-beat silence passed.

'You are very bitter,' he observed.

'I've lost almost six years of my life,' she bit out. 'Do you know what that feels like, Sebastian? The world is suddenly a different place. I feel like I don't belong anywhere any more.'

'You killed your father, Cassie,' he reminded her. 'I am not sure what led you to do that, but the laws of this island dictate you must pay for that in some way. There are many people on Aristo who feel you have been given a very lenient sentence.'

'Yes, well, they didn't know my father, did they?' she shot back without thinking.

His frown deepened. 'Your father was well respected in all quarters. What are you saying…that he was not the private man we all knew in public?'

Cassie wished she could have pulled her words back. She had revealed far more than she had intended to. She had told no one of her father's behaviour over the years. Who would believe her if she had? It was a secret, a dirty secret that she alone had lived with. Shame had always kept her silent and it would continue to do so. Besides, she hadn't done herself any favours behaving like a spoilt brat for most of her life. Her father had played on that for all it was worth, publicly tearing his hair out over her behaviour to all his well-connected friends and colleagues.

Cassie quickly averted her gaze, and, shuffling in her bag,

drew out the picture Sam had drawn in a desperate attempt to change the subject. 'Um…I almost forgot to give you this,' she said, handing it to him with fingers that made the paper give a betraying rattle. 'One of the…er…orphans drew it for you. He insisted I give it to you.'

He took the picture and gently unfolded it, his eyes taking in the childish strokes of pencil and brightly coloured crayons. 'It is very…nice,' he said and brought his gaze back to hers. 'You said this child is without parents?'

Cassie looked at him blankly for a moment.

'Um…well…I…he's…'

'The child is a boy?'

'Yes.'

'And an orphan.' He looked back at the drawing, his brows moving together over his eyes. 'How old is he?' he asked, looking back at her again.

Cassie felt as if his eyes were burning a pathway to her soul. 'He's…five or thereabouts,' she said, shifting her gaze once more.

'Too young to be all alone in the world,' Sebastian said with deep compassion in his tone. 'Do you know anything of his background, where he came from, who his parents were or what happened to them?'

The hole Cassie had dug for herself was getting bigger by the moment. She could feel the fast pace of panic throughout her body, making her heart thump unevenly and her skin break out in fine beads of perspiration, some of which were even now beginning to trickle down between her shoulder blades.

'Cassie?'

'Um…' She brushed a strand of hair off her face as she returned her eyes to his, the stutter of her heart painful in her chest. 'I'm not sure of the details of every individual child's background. All I know is the children at the Aristo orphanage are there because they don't have anywhere else to go.'

Sebastian laid the picture on a sideboard as if it were a priceless work of art. 'I am very touched that a small abandoned child would take the time to do this for me,' he said in a tone that was gravel-rough. 'I have lived with nothing but privilege all my life so it is hard for me to imagine what it must be like to have no one you can turn to, especially when one is so young.'

Damn right it is, Cassie silently agreed.

He turned and looked directly at her. 'I would like to meet this child,' he said. 'I would like to thank him personally.'

Cassie felt as if her eyes were going to pop out of her head and land on the carpeted floor at his feet. She looked at him in abject horror, her mouth opening and closing like a stranded fish, her heart going so hard and fast it felt as if it were going to come through the wall of her chest. 'I—I'm not sure that can be arranged,' she stammered.

He gave her a frowning look. 'I fail to see why not. After all, I am now the royal patron of the orphanage. It is only reasonable and fair that I give my support in ways other than financial.'

'Y-yes, but showing preference for one child over another is not to be advised,' Cassie said, relieved she could think of something reasonably plausible on the spot. 'The child who sent you this drawing is one of many who long to be noticed. You would be doing more harm than good singling any one of them out over another.'

His gaze was still unwavering on hers. 'What if I were to invite all the children to a special party at the palace?' he suggested. 'That way no one will feel left out.'

'Um…I…I…' she choked as her self-made petard gave her another sharp poke.

'At the gala it occurred to me that the most important people were not at the event—the children themselves,' he went on. 'I had a word to my events secretary about arranging something last night.'

Cassie was still trying to get her voice to cooperate. 'Um…is that such a good idea?' she asked. 'The kids might be a little intimidated by the palace… I mean, royal protocol is off-putting enough for adults…'

'My father had a hands-off approach when it came to the organisations he put his name to,' he said. 'I intend to do things differently, and what better place to start than the orphanage right on the palace doorstep?'

'It's hardly on the doorstep,' Cassie said. 'It's practically attached to the prison.'

He rubbed at his jaw for a moment. 'Yes, that is true. But that is something I would like to discuss with you over lunch.' He pulled out one of the chairs next to the small dining table. 'Would you care to sit down?'

'Thank you,' Cassie said, immensely glad of the seat as her legs were still trembling out of control.

She watched as he took his own seat, his longs legs brushing against hers under the table. She drew in a quick, unsteady breath and moved her legs back, but she could still sense the heat and strength of his in close proximity to hers.

Sebastian rang a small bell, and within seconds the aide appeared pushing a trolley with several covered dishes as well as iced water and a bottle of chilled white wine.

Cassie sat fidgeting with the neck of her uniform as the aide served them both the light lunch of char-grilled octopus and a Greek salad and fresh crusty rolls.

'Would you care for some wine, Dhespinis Kyriakis?'

'No…thank you,' she said. 'Water will be fine. Thank you.'

'Thank you, Stefanos,' Sebastian said once his wine and Cassie's water had been poured. 'Has a date been confirmed for the event we discussed?'

'Yes, Your Highness,' Stefanos said and handed Sebastian a slip of paper. 'Your diary has been cleared.'

Sebastian glanced down at the date on the paper before he folded it and slipped it into the breast pocket of his shirt. 'That was very efficient of you, Stefanos,' he said. 'Well done.'

The aide bowed respectfully and left the room, closing the door softly but firmly behind him.

Sebastian picked up his glass of wine, twirling it in his hand for a moment as he centred his gaze on Cassie. 'You do not drink alcohol any more, Cassie?' he asked.

Cassie looked at the tiny condensation bubbles clinging to the outside of his crystal glass and wondered if she would ever be able to look at alcohol again without feeling shame. In the past she had done so many things while inebriated she would never have done normally. She cringed at the thought of how she had come across to so many people, Sebastian included. She had always been the life of the party, laughing and care-free as drink after drink had been consumed. Her worries had lessened with every mouthful and, even though the head-aches the next morning had been unpleasant, she had been prepared to put up with some discomfort for the temporary reprieve the consumption of alcohol had given her.

She was suddenly conscious of the stretching silence and Sebastian's steady dark gaze on her. 'I lost my taste for alcohol while I was in prison,' she said quietly. 'I haven't touched it since.'

'That is probably a good thing,' he said. 'I don't drink as much as I did when I was young. I guess we have grown up, *ne?* A glass of wine at lunch or dinner is plenty.'

'Do you ever see any of the gang we used to hang around with?' Cassie asked once they had commenced eating the de-licious salad.

'The brat-pack?' he asked with a ghost of a wistful smile.

Cassie nodded, thinking of the hip crowd and the hangers-on they had associated with six years ago. She could almost guarantee she had been the only one to end up with a criminal record. The others were like Sebastian, out to have fun until family duty called. Not like she, who had been looking for something to take her mind off what she couldn't quite face…

'I see a few of them, of course, do business occasionally with them,' Sebastian said, and then smiled. 'I do not see so much of Odessa Tsoulis. Last I heard she had married a billionaire from Texas.'

Cassie felt a small smile tug at her mouth. 'She was rather intent on landing herself a rich husband, if I recall.'

'Yes, indeed,' Sebastian said with a small laugh. 'She was good fun. I liked her. She was very no-nonsense if you know what I mean. What you saw was what you got.'

'Unlike me.' Cassie wasn't sure why she had said it, much less how she was going to deal with it now it was said. She looked away from his suddenly penetrating gaze, and, picking up her fork with a tiny rattle against the plate, resumed eating, but with little appetite.

'Tell me about it, Cassie,' he pressed her gently. 'Tell me what happened that night.'

Cassie stared at one of the octopus curls on her plate and wished herself a thousand miles away. Why couldn't he leave the past where it belonged? What good did it do to haul over the ice-cold coals of regret? She couldn't change anything. That had been the problem in the first place.

She couldn't change anything.

'I'd rather not talk about it,' she said, and put her fork down with another little clatter against the edge of the plate.

'Did you have an argument or something?' he asked.

'Or something,' she said with a curl of her lip. 'I said leave it, Sebastian. It's done with. I don't like being reminded of it.'

'It must have been terrifying for you to be carted off to prison like that,' he said, clearly determined to keep pressing her.

Cassie gave him a resentful look. 'I didn't happen to see you in the crowd to offer me your support.'

His expression darkened. 'Would you have accepted my support if I had offered it?' he asked. 'You told me never to contact you again, remember? In any case I went abroad for several months after you ended our affair. I didn't hear much about what was going on and no one in my family thought to tell me because they didn't even know of our involvement. By the time I got back my father had already warned Lissa never to contact you and had packed her off to university in Paris before she could utter a single word of protest.'

'So when you did get back you let me rot in prison because you didn't want your father to find out we'd had an affair,' she said bitterly.

'Wrong!' He was only a decibel or two away from shouting the word at her. 'Cassie, why can't you see this from my point of view?'

Cassie got up from the table, pushing in her chair with such force it sent a shock wave through his wineglass, the alcohol spilling over the edges and onto the crisp white tablecloth. 'Oh, I can see this from your point of view, all right,' she snipped at him. 'A few months ago I was just yet another nameless person locked away in prison. Someone from your past you didn't dare speak about, much less step forward and defend. Now you find I am one of the key players at the orphanage you want to support, so you think it might be timely to pour oil over troubled waters to mollify me enough to maintain your reputation in case I spill all to the press about our little clandestine affair.'

'I care nothing for my reputation,' he ground out with a flintlike flash of his dark eyes. 'It is my family I am concerned about. I owe it to the generations of Karedes who have gone before me to act in a manner fitting for a future king.'

She rolled her eyes at him. 'So I guess that's why we aren't having lunch where everyone can see us, right, Sebastian? To maintain your family's honour.'

His brow was still deeply furrowed. 'I was thinking of your safety. I told you last night there are still many people in the community who think you should have got life in prison.'

'I did get life!' Cassie said, closer to tears than she had been in years. 'Do you think this is ever going to go away? I am marked for life as the daughter who killed her father. I see the way people look at me. They even cross to the other side of the road rather than look me in the eye. Don't tell me I haven't already been punished enough. Just don't tell me.'

He stepped towards her but she moved away, holding up a hand like a barrier to ward him off. 'Please…' She was close to begging and hated herself for it. 'Give me a moment…*please*…'

Sebastian clenched his hands to stop them reaching for her. He wanted to comfort her, to tell her things would improve now she was free, but he wasn't sure she wanted to hear such platitudes from him. In any case, he wasn't entirely sure they held any truth. But he'd also wanted to tell her how deeply shocked he had been to hear of her father's death and the charge of murder she had been landed with. He could not believe his Caz could have done such a thing. But then he hadn't thought her capable of the black-hearted deceit she had informed him of the day prior to her father's death.

She had gone from his bed to one of her many lovers, probably laughing about him behind his back the whole time. His gut still churned thinking about it, even after all this time. She wasn't the person he had fallen in love with. He realised in hindsight the person he had loved was a fantasy he had constructed in his head. He had been a fool not to see her for what she was. She had acted the part of the devoted lover so easily and he had fallen for it. She was like a chameleon, changing constantly to fit in with the company or each situation she found herself in.

But who was Cassandra Kyriakis now? She had spent five years in prison and another eleven months on parole, an experience any young woman would find life-changing, hopefully even reforming in some way. In any case, her days of living off her father's wealth were long gone. Theo's estate had been divided up between distant relatives, leaving Cassie virtually penniless. While her father had been alive, Cassie had spent his money as if entitled to every euro of it.

Each time Sebastian had dared to bring up the subject of her taking a career or job of her own she had laughed in his face, telling him she was having a perfectly fine time living the life of a socialite.

Cassie appeared to enjoy her work at the orphanage now, but what would happen when her parole period was up? Sebastian had had enough trouble adjusting to living constantly in the public eye, but how much worse would it be for Cassie with the shame of her father's death hanging over her?

CHAPTER FOUR

CASSIE composed herself with an effort and resumed her seat at the table as if nothing had happened. She picked up her glass of water and drank several mouthfuls, conscious of Sebastian looking at her with a frown beetling his brows.

She set her glass back down. 'You said you had something to discuss with me over lunch about the orphanage,' she reminded him coolly, and pointedly looked at her watch, making it clear she was on a strict time line, and, more to the point, he was not important enough to her to adjust it to accommodate him.

He came back to the table and sat down, his expression still brooding. 'You switch it on and off like magic, don't you, Cassie?' he said.

She sent him an indifferent look without answering.

'Damn it, Cassie, for once in your life show me you're human,' he growled at her. 'You never let anyone get close to you.'

Cassie clenched her hands into hard fists of tension in her lap and glared at him across the table. 'What do you want me to do, Sebastian? Weep and wail and gnash my teeth? Would that make you feel better? To think I'm an emotional wreck, crippled by guilt and unable to resume my place in the world?'

His eyes travelled over her face, pausing for a moment on

the tight line of her mouth before locking on her flinty gaze. 'I am not sure what I want from you, to tell you the truth,' he said heavily.

'Perhaps that's why you invited me here,' Cassie went on in the same resentful and embittered tone, 'to have a gawk at me, a real-life prisoner. I guess not too many prince regents get the opportunity to have a private meeting with an ex-criminal.'

His mouth tightened. 'It's not like that at all, Cassie,' he said.

'Then what is it like, Sebastian?' she asked. 'Why am I here?'

He held her feisty look, his dark gaze sombre. 'I wanted to see you again. To make sure you are all right.' He released a breath in a small sigh and added, 'I guess to see if you had changed.'

Cassie cocked one eyebrow at him. 'And what is your verdict?'

He surveyed her features for several seconds, each one seeming like an eternity to Cassie under his ever-tightening scrutiny.

'It's hard to say,' he said at last. 'You look the same, you even sound the same, but something tells me you are very different.'

'The correction services people will be very glad to hear that,' she quipped without humour. 'What a waste of public money if my incarceration hadn't had some effect on my rebellious character.'

His eyes held hers for another moment or two. 'You still don't like yourself, though, do you, Cassie?'

Cassie forced herself to keep her gaze trained on his, but it cost her dearly. She felt her defences crumbling and hoped she could hold herself together until she was alone. 'I am quite at home with who I am,' she said. 'Like a lot of people, I have things I don't like about myself, but no one's perfect.'

'What don't you like about yourself?'

She chewed on her bottom lip and then, realising he was

watching her, quickly released it. 'I don't like my…er…feet,' she said, suddenly stuck for an answer. 'I have ugly feet.'

His mouth tilted in a smile. 'You have beautiful feet, *agape mou,*' he said. 'How can you think they are not?'

'I think they're too big,' she said. 'I would like dainty feet like my mother had. I found a pair of her shoes one day but I could barely get my big toe in. She was so beautiful, so petite and elegant.'

'I saw one or two photographs of her in your father's office when I accompanied my father one time,' he said. 'She was indeed very lovely, but you are exactly like her.'

Cassie picked up her water glass so she could break his gaze. 'I sometimes wonder if we would have got on…you know…if she had lived.'

'I am sure you would have enjoyed a close relationship,' he said. 'There is something about a mother's love. My mother is much softer than my father ever was. He ruled with an iron fist but my mother was an expert in shaping our behaviour with positive attention and positive and loving feedback.'

'She must have taken your father's death very hard,' Cassie said and, biting her lip again, added, 'I am sorry I didn't express my condolences to you before now. I should have said something last night.'

'Do not trouble yourself,' he said. 'It was a dreadful shock, yes, especially as it happened on the night of my mother's sixtieth birthday party.'

'Yes, I heard about that,' she said, looking up at him again. 'A heart attack, wasn't it?'

He gave a grim nod. 'All my life I have been groomed for the position of taking my father's place when he died. I have developed a strong sense of duty as a result. This island is my home. The people who live here are my people. The only thing

I am having trouble with now is I did not expect the responsibility to be passed on quite so soon.'

'Yes…yes, of course,' she said softly.

'But enough about that for now,' he said with a stiff smile that didn't quite involve his eyes. 'I wanted to talk to you about the orphanage. It seems an odd position for it to be located next to the prison, don't you think?'

'It is, but there's never been any problem as far as I know,' Cassie said. 'And with the prison having its own crèche it makes it easier for female prisoners with babies and young children to have them on site with them.'

A frown wrinkled his forehead. 'You mean there are some women who have children in prison with them while they serve their sentence?'

Cassie kept her eyes on his even though she could feel her face heating. 'Yes…but only until the child is three years old. After that they are usually fostered out until the mother's sentence comes to an end.'

'But is prison really the best place for an infant or toddler?' he asked, still with a frown in place.

'The best place for any small child is with its mother,' Cassie said. 'The child hasn't done anything wrong. Why should it be separated from its mother at such a young and vulnerable age?'

'Is that what happened to the little boy who drew me that picture?'

Cassie lowered her eyes and reached for her water glass again. 'I told you I'm not familiar with every child's circumstances, but, yes, it could well be that he has been taken away from his mother and that he had nowhere else to go. Relatives are not always well placed to take on someone else's child, especially a child whose mother is serving time in prison.'

A small silence fell into the space between them. Cassie

could hear it ringing in her ears, her heart thudding so loudly she could feel the blood tingling in her fingertips where she was holding on to her glass. She forced herself to relax, making her shoulders soften from their stiffly held position, taking a moment to concentrate on breathing evenly and deeply to establish some semblance of calm.

'I am uncomfortable with the notion of an infant under three being housed along with violent criminals,' he said. 'The same arrangement would not for a moment be considered in a male prison.'

'Yes, that is true, but there are very good reasons for that,' Cassie said. 'For one, almost ninety per cent of female prisoners are jailed for non-violent crimes. They are far more commonly in for drug abuse or drug-related offences to feed their habit. They are very often the victims of childhood abuse and fall into the no-win cycle of drugs to help them cope with the devastation of their lives. Also, people now recognise the important bonding that goes on with an infant and its mother.'

'You grew close to some of those women?' he asked, appearing genuinely interested.

'It is hard not to in such a confined place,' Cassie said, thinking of the lifelong friends she had made, including Angelica. 'The loss of dignity hits hard, not to mention the loss of freedom. Counting the days off the calendar can be a very lonely task unless you have someone to talk to.'

'Will you be able to move on from this?' he asked softly.

'I would like to think so,' she said with a small measure of carefully nurtured confidence. 'Once my parole is up I want to leave Aristo and start afresh.'

'What will you do?'

'I am a bit limited given my criminal record,' Cassie said. 'Not many employers want an ex-prisoner on their books. But I would like to study. I wasted my time at school so the thought of doing my leaving certificate again is tempting. After that, who knows? As long as it brings in enough money to put food on the table for us…I mean, for me, I'll be happy.'

'I heard your father did not leave you well provided for.'

Cassie gave him a twisted look. 'No, funny that, don't you think? He left everything he owned to some distant cousins twice removed. He must have known I was going to push him down the stairs that night.'

'What happened, Cassie?' he asked again, looking at her intently.

Cassie dropped her gaze from his. 'We argued,' she said in a flat emotionless tone. 'I hardly remember what we argued about now—it all seems so muddled and foggy in my head. He was shouting at me, I was shouting back at him and then…' She closed her eyes tight, mentally skipping over that distressing scene until she felt she had control again. She reopened her eyes and carried on as if discussing the weekend weather. 'Suddenly he was lying at the foot of the staircase with a head wound.'

'What did you do?'

'I panicked,' she said, frowning as she forced herself to remember what had happened next. 'I tried to get him to stand up. I thought he was putting it on just to scare me but he…' she swallowed '…he didn't…he didn't wake up…'

'So the police came and arrested you?'

She shook her head. 'Not at first. They treated it as an accidental death, but a few weeks later one of the neighbours came forward and testified to hearing us arguing that night. Apparently that was enough to set the ball rolling. Within a few hours I was handcuffed and dragged off to give a statement. I pleaded guilty to manslaughter early the following day.' *Because I didn't have the strength to fight after being hounded and questioned for hours by the police and no one would believe me if I told them the truth in any case,* Cassie added silently. The interview room had been full of her father's cronies. What chance had she had to clear her name?

'It must have been terrifying for you,' Sebastian said, his voice sounding as if it had been dragged over something rough. 'You were only eighteen years old.'

'It is over now,' she said. 'I have many regrets over how things were handled, but the police were only doing their job. My father was a high-profile man. People wanted their scape-goat and I was it.'

'What are you saying, Cassie? That you were forced into confessing to a crime you did not commit?' he asked with a heavy frown.

Here's your chance, Cassie thought. *Tell him what it was like. Tell him everything.* She even got as far as opening her mouth but the words wouldn't come out. If she told him about her father she would have to tell him about Sam. What if Sebastian and his family decided she was not a good enough mother for a royal prince? Sam had already been wrenched out of her arms when he was little more than a baby; he would be devastated to have it happen again, even though he was close to school age. If he was taken away from her a second time her devastation would be complete. The only reason she had survived the hell of the last six years had been because of her love for her little boy. To have come this far and lose him at the last hurdle was unthinkable.

'Cassie?'

'No,' she said, addressing his left shoulder rather than his all-seeing gaze. 'No, of course I wasn't forced. I understood what was going on and agreed to accept the lesser charge of manslaughter.'

'Did you have good legal representation?' he asked.

Cassie thought of the sleazy lawyer she had been assigned.

During each of the long drawn-out weeks of the trial he had looked at her as if she had been sitting there naked, his snake-like eyes sliding all over her, reminding her so much of that last altercation with her father she would have agreed to a charge of murder if it had meant she could be free of the lawyer's loathsome presence all the sooner.

'I had a lawyer,' she said tonelessly. 'We didn't exactly hit it off, but beggars can't be choosers, right?'

Sebastian felt another knifelike twist of guilt assail him at her tone. He knew there was a lot she wasn't telling him, but he could read between the lines enough to know a competent lawyer should have been able to get her off given her age at the time. What if she had acted in self-defence? Surely she shouldn't have been punished under those circumstances?

But then he thought of the rumours that had been going round at the time of Theo Kyriakis's death. Rumours of Theo's increasing despair over his wayward daughter's drug and alcohol problems. Sebastian knew about Cassie's drinking but he had never seen her using or acting under the influence of drugs. That didn't mean she hadn't been using them, of course. Drug addicts were notoriously adept at keeping secrets. She could easily have popped any number of pills when he wasn't with her. Their time together had been limited in any case. Keeping their relationship a secret had been his idea; he hadn't wanted the interference of his overbearing father, not to mention the ever-present paparazzi.

Once Sebastian had found out about Cassie's betrayal he'd had good reason to be glad their relationship had been such a closely guarded secret. It had been bad enough imagining her laughing at him, let alone the whole population of Aristo. But even so, sometimes he wondered if he had done the right thing.

He had never mentioned it to anyone, but Theo Kyriakis had often struck Sebastian as a little too suave and smooth talking for his liking. He couldn't quite put his finger on it, but there had been something about the man he hadn't warmed to as others—including his father—had done. For instance, if Theo had been such a loving and concerned father, why on earth had his will been written in such a way unless he had known Cassie was going to kill him, as she had hinted at only moments ago? It didn't make sense. What made even less sense was why the lawyer defending her hadn't pointed that out at the time.

'How are you managing for money now?' Sebastian asked.

A glitter of pride flashed in her gaze as it met his. 'I'm fine. I have what I need for…for myself.'

Sebastian wondered if she was telling the truth. There was something about her that suggested she was more than a little uncomfortable in his presence. She never used to shift her gaze and gnaw at her bottom lip in that restive manner. But then perhaps her time in prison had made her wary of people. It was understandable considering what he had heard about life in prison. He didn't like to think about what she must have suffered. There was no secret about the violence and rivalry behind bars, even in women's prisons. Drug use was rife, vicious hierarchies existed and corruption amongst guards was commonplace. No wonder she was edgy and unable to relax even for a moment.

She looked at her watch and got to her feet. 'I have to go,' she said. 'My lunch hour is almost up.'

He intercepted her before she had even picked up her purse off the floor. 'No, Cassie,' he said, placing one of his hands over her forearm. 'I have not finished talking to you yet.'

Cassie looked down at his tanned fingers lying across her bare arm and gave an involuntary shiver. Those hands had taught her so much about passion. They had explored every contour of her body. And for close to six years she had dreamt of how it would feel to have them touch her again. The way he had touched and kissed her last night had made her all the more vulnerable to him. She didn't have the courage to look at his face, for she was sure he would see the longing there in her eyes. She ached with it; it was like a taut thread in her body, tightening unbearably every time she was near him, pulling her inexorably closer to him.

'Look at me, Cassie,' he said into the thrumming silence.

She swallowed and slowly brought her eyes to his. 'I really have to go, Sebastian,' she said. 'Some of the younger children have naps after lunch and I always read to them. They will become agitated if I'm not there.' She took a tiny swallow and added, 'I don't like letting them down.'

'I told my secretary to inform the director you would not be back until three at the latest.'

She narrowed her eyes at him. *'You did what?'*

His fingers moved down her arm to encircle her wrist, bringing her closer to his hard, tall frame. 'I cleared my diary so we could have this time together.'

'You had no right to interfere like that!' Cassie said, tugging at his hold to no avail. She felt herself climb yet another unstable rung on the ladder of her panic. She could see her little son's worried face at the window, waiting for her. She could hear the nervous staccato of his speech as he asked Sophie or Kara where his mummy was. She could even see the puddle on the floor and his wet pants, which would distress Sam even though he couldn't help it during times of acute stress.

'Why all the fuss?' Sebastian asked, still holding her firmly. 'Surely you have earned a couple of hours off?'

Cassie tried to prise off his fingers but he placed his other hand over hers, a move she had no hope of counteracting. She gulped in a ragged breath as she brought her eyes to his. His dark eyes became even darker as they centred on her mouth, the touch of his fingers going from firm and restraining to gentle and tantalisingly sensual. The drugging movement of his thumb on the underside of her wrist caused the slow but inexorable melt of her bones and what was left of her resistance. The blood in her veins became hectic under the rapid-fire beat of her heart. Her stomach felt hollow, her legs felt weak and her breathing became shallow and uneven as his warm breath skated over the surface of her lips as his head came down…

The first brushlike stroke of his mouth on hers was tentative, even a little hesitant, a bit like a goose feather, so soft she wondered if she had imagined it. The second was firmer, with a hint of growing urgency, but the third tasted of desire hot and strong, rocking Cassie to the core. She opened her mouth to the searching glide of his tongue, her insides turning to jelly when that deliciously erotic contact was made. The kiss became more urgent, more passionate, more out of control and she was swept away with it. It felt so wonderful to be held in his arms again, to have his hands at her waist, holding her trembling body against the heat and strength of his. He was hard and getting harder as every second passed, the hollow ache in her body echoing the pounding of his blood against her.

His hands moved from her waist to the small of her back, bringing her closer to his surging heat. Cassie felt her body moisten and her stomach did another dip and dive at the thought of how it had felt with him deep inside her in the past, the rocking motion of their bodies bringing them to the ultimate moment in human pleasure. It was like a craving he had started within her and no one else could ever satisfy it but him. The thought of sharing her body with anyone else was abhorrent to her and had been from the first time she had experienced pleasure in his arms. She had resigned herself to a lifetime of celibacy, never dreaming that one day he would come back into her life and want her again.

He lifted his mouth off hers, his eyes blazing as they locked on hers. 'I want you and I intend to have you again even if it is only for one night. Think about it, Cassie. One night to remember for the rest of our lives.'

'This can't happen, Sebastian,' she whispered hoarsely even as she felt her body sway towards him. 'You know it can't. We were worlds apart before. Now we live in different universes.'

He traced the outline of her cupid's bow with the tip of his index finger. 'My head is telling me that but not the rest of me. Why do you do this to me, Cassie? Have you cast a spell on me?'

'Please don't make this any harder than it already is,' she pleaded with him. 'Let me go, Sebastian, before we do something we will not just remember, but quite possibly regret for the rest of our lives.'

He cupped her face in his hands, locking her gaze with his. 'No one needs to know about it but us.'

Cassie's heart gave another head-spinning lurch. 'You're really serious about this…'

His thumbs began caressing the twin curves of her cheeks, his eyes so dark she couldn't see his pupils. 'I want you, Caz. I still want you. As soon as I saw you at the gala last night I knew I would not rest until I had you again. After we kissed…well, that confirmed to me that you felt the same.'

'Sebastian…' She tried to inject some implacability to her tone but she wasn't sure she quite pulled it off. 'There are lots of things in life people want but it doesn't mean they can have them. This will never work between us. You're the Prince Regent of Aristo and I am…well, you know what I am… everyone knows what I am…'

'What does it matter what you are or what you have done?'

he asked. 'This is about here and now, not the future. I cannot offer you marriage, you know that, and, if what you said in the past is true, you don't want me to. I am offering you an affair to satisfy our needs, that is all.'

Cassie dipped out of his hold and put some distance between them. 'This is crazy, Sebastian.' She rubbed at her upper arms as if warding off a chill. 'You kept our relationship a secret last time but only just. The threat of exposure was constant. How much worse will it be now? Everyone watches your every move. The paparazzi are like ants at a picnic. The guards you surround yourself with could so easily be bribed for a price on your comings and goings. You are no longer in a position to control your public life, let alone your private one.'

'I have ways and means to keep some aspects of my life absolutely private,' he countered. 'I have chosen my personal staff very carefully. They would not betray me. I am absolutely sure of it.'

'This…this thing between us is just about sex,' she said in rising frustration. 'Do you have any idea how that makes me feel?'

He gave her an ironic look. 'Feelings, Cassie?' he said. 'What is this? What happened to the I-just-want-to-have-fun-without-strings Cassie Kyriakis of the past, hmm?'

She never existed in the first place, Cassie said to herself and dearly wished she could say it out loud. She had constructed a fantasy to keep people from seeing the real Cassie. Who would want the real deal? Even her father, her only living relative, had not been able to look at her without hatred and disgust glittering in his eyes.

'I want different things now,' she said, trying to control the slight wobble in her voice. 'I have spent a long time thinking about where I went wrong. I don't want to make the same mistakes this time around.'

A glint of resentment lit his gaze as it pinned hers. 'So you consider your involvement with me back then as a mistake?'

Cassie thought of her little son. *Their* little son. How could she regret the one good thing, the *only* good thing that had come out of their short-lived and secret relationship? Sam was everything to her. He was her saviour, her reason for living. She could never, not in a million years, regret anything to do with how he was conceived. 'No…' she said at the end of an expelled breath. 'I went into our relationship with my eyes wide open.'

'Not to mention your legs.'

She flinched as if he had struck her. 'I beg your pardon?'

'Come on, Cassie,' he said with a derisive look. 'You were no blushing virgin when you leapt into my bed.'

She ground her teeth as she fought to contain her temper. 'That's a rather sexist thing to say. You had plenty of experience yourself, if I remember correctly.'

'But still not enough for you,' he said with a cutting edge to his tone. 'You had God knows how many other men lining up to pleasure you. You gave me a list of names, remember?'

Each and every lie she had ever told seemed determined to backfire on her one way or the other. The only thing she could do was to paper over her previous lies with more lies and hope to God he never discovered the truth. 'I am not particularly proud of my behaviour back then,' she said stiffly, 'but you never gave me any indication you were developing more serious feelings for me. I thought we wanted the same things—fun without strings.'

'It started that way, yes, but you had a rather bewitching way about you, Cassie, that made me want more,' he said. 'I was going to tell you but you got in first with your announcement that you wanted out.'

Cassie stared at him, her heart sinking at the thought of

what she had inadvertently thrown away. Why hadn't he given her some clue earlier? She had never for a moment suspected he was falling for her. He had been very passionate and attentive, yes, but as for showing any sign of developing stronger feelings... Oh, dear God! What cruel twist of fate had led them to this torturous impasse?

The silence stretched and stretched to the point of agony.

'Aren't you going to ask me, Cassie?' Sebastian said.

She shook herself out of her frozen state. 'Ask you w-what?'

His top lip curled sardonically. 'The question women always ask in situations such as this.'

Cassie pressed her lips together as she struggled with her see-sawing emotions. 'OK, then...' She took an unsteady breath and asked him even though she knew it would not help her to know, but rather would only make it a thousand times worse. 'Do you still have feelings for me?'

He stood looking at her for a long time before answering. Cassie wondered if he was still making up his mind. But in the end she wasn't all that surprised by his answer—heart-wrenchingly disappointed, yes, but not a bit surprised.

'I do not love you,' he said. 'Do not mistake physical desire for more noble feelings. There is nothing noble or indeed proper about what I feel for you now, Cassie. I want an affair with you to get you out of my system before I take up the reins of duty. I will be expected to marry and to marry well. I believe someone has already been earmarked as a potential bride.'

Cassie felt as if he had plunged a serrated fishing knife deep into her chest. She wanted to bend over double to counteract the pain but only pride kept her upright and rigid. 'Oh, really?' she said in a disinterested tone. 'That certainly takes the legwork out for you, doesn't it? Just think—no hours wasted flirting, no money thrown away on flowers and meals at exclusive restaurants. Lucky you.'

His eyes were dark slits of brooding anger. 'This is not over, Cassie,' he said. 'Not by a long shot. I would not have brought you here if I did not believe you want the same thing as I do. You betrayed it to me last night when you returned my kiss.'

'Yes, well, that's only because I haven't been kissed for a long…' Cassie stopped and bit her lip, suddenly realising she had just tripped over one of her very own lies…

CHAPTER FIVE

SEBASTIAN came across to where she was standing, and, taking her chin between his thumb and index finger, lifted her face to meet his gaze. 'So there is no current man in your life,' he mused. 'What other lies have you told me, hmm?'

Cassie felt her heart kicking erratically behind her chest wall. Her mouth dried up, her throat locked tight and her breathing came to a shuddering halt. 'Just that one…' she said, mentally calculating how many falsehoods she had told him within the space of less than twenty-four hours.

'I wonder what other little secrets you are keeping,' he said, still holding her gaze with the piercing scrutiny of his. 'Like where you live, for instance.'

Cassie swallowed. 'Where I live is no secret.'

'If so, then why was it when Stefanos dropped you at your house last night you failed to enter it but slipped out of sight up a lane before he could follow you?'

'Um…I…'

He smiled at her knowingly. 'Are you frightened Aristo's future king might call around for a spontaneous visit, hmm?'

You bet I am, Cassie thought in stomach-lurching dread. 'I'm sure you are far too busy to make house calls to commoners, much less ex-criminals,' she said, her tongue darting out to moisten her bone-dry lips. 'Besides, you wouldn't dream of drawing press attention to yourself in such a way.'

His thumb began stroking the underside of her chin, back and forth in a movement that was as potent as a mind-altering drug. 'I am tempted to risk it,' he said, looking at her mouth. 'For you, *agape mou,* I think I would be tempted to risk a great deal.'

Cassie felt another shock wave of reaction roll through her. 'You don't mean that…' she said. 'You hate me for…for betraying you. Why would you risk your reputation and your credibility for someone like me?'

He picked up a strand of her hair and tucked it behind her ear. 'Why indeed?'

'Sebastian…' she said raggedly as she put a hand on his chest to hold him back.

His much larger and broader hand covered hers, almost swallowing it whole. 'One night, Caz,' he said in a husky voice. 'Just give me one night.'

Cassie scrunched her eyes tightly shut to ward off the overwhelming temptation of being in his arms again. 'Sebastian…' *I want to, oh, how I want to!* She was so dangerously close to confessing. How could he not see it? The temptation he was dangling in front of her was overwhelming. To have one night with him, one night to keep her going for the rest of her life would be a glimpse of heaven.

'Look at me, Cassie,' he said softly but no less commandingly.

She slowly opened her eyes. His were impossibly dark and surprisingly soft; as if somewhere deep inside there was a part of him that had not yet exchanged his love for her for hate. Would one night reawaken everything he had felt for her in the past? Or would it do as he hoped and expunge her from his system once and for all?

'You're asking too much,' she said in a scratchy whisper. 'Way, way too much.'

'I want to feel it again, Cassie,' he said, running his hands down her bare arms to encircle her wrists. 'Remember what it was like between us?'

Cassie remembered too well, that was half the trouble. Hardly a day went by when she didn't think of the explosive magic she had felt in his arms. She had not known her body could respond so feverishly and so uninhibitedly until he had made her his. Her one brief foray into physical intimacy with another lover when she was seventeen had nowhere near prepared her for the cataclysmic response Sebastian's touch evoked. Even now with his long fingers curled around the slender bones of her wrists she felt the power and potency of him through the fine layers of her skin. She ached with the memories of his lovemaking, the way he had made her beg for release at times; she had almost screamed at him, tearing at him with her fingers until he had thrust her through the door to physical paradise. Oh, the pleasure she had felt in his arms! Shivers skated down her spine as she recalled just even one erotic moment of being possessed by him.

'You can't tell me it was like that for you with other men,' he continued when she didn't answer. 'I have had lovers before and after you, Cassie, and it was never the same. There is amazing chemistry between us. It makes everything else pale in comparison.'

'You're chasing a fantasy, Sebastian,' she said. 'We've both changed. We're not the same people now.'

'We might have changed but this is one thing that certainly hasn't,' he said, and, swooping down, covered her mouth with the crushing urgency of his.

Cassie knew she should pull out of his hold. There were a hundred reasons to push him away, but somehow she couldn't quite do it. The moment his lips met hers she felt the rush of need consume her. Her senses leapt with each stroke and glide of his masterful tongue, reducing her to a quivering wreck within moments. Was there no cure for this madness? she wondered dizzily. Everything about him felt so right and perfect. The pressure of his kiss, the movement of his hands from her wrists to her waist, then to just beneath her breasts, not quite touching but near enough to make them start to tingle and swell in anticipation.

She whimpered as his mouth continued to ruthlessly and passionately plunder hers, the lascivious dart of his tongue sending her crazy with the need to feel him in that secret heart of her that throbbed and ached for his possession. She leaned into his tight embrace, her arms going around his neck, her fingers threading through his thick dark hair as she returned his kiss with an ardour that more than matched his.

'You still want me,' Sebastian growled against her mouth, barely lifting his lips high enough to get the words out. 'I can taste it in every kiss we have shared.'

Cassie shivered as his warm breath fanned her swollen lips and she opened her eyes and looked up at him dazedly. 'I've always wanted you...'

One of his hands cupped her breast, cradling its gentle weight while the pad of his thumb began to roll over her engorged nipple. 'I swore I would never allow you to reduce me to this again,' he said, nibbling at the lobe of her ear with knee-wobbling deftness. 'But I can't help it. When I am with you I feel like I am going to burst like a trigger-happy teenager.'

Cassie felt the hardened probe of his erection pressing into her belly and felt a wave of desire wash over her, leaving her trembling with the force of it. She reached for him, her fingers skating over the waistband of his trousers before they went lower.

He groaned at the back of his throat as she outlined his rigid form through the fabric of his trousers, his reaction inciting her to roll down his zipper. He sucked in a breath, his hands on her ribcage grasping at her for purchase as she gently peeled his underwear away.

She could smell the erotic musk of his arousal, the skin stretched so tightly over his length her fingers trembled as she stroked him. He was so strong and powerful and yet her caressing touch brought him to life in a way she found totally exhilarating.

He groaned again, the deep, almost primitive sound fanning the flames of her desire for him. 'You have to stop, Cassie,' he said between ragged breaths. 'I can't take any more.'

Cassie ignored his plea and continued to caress him, but his hands came down on her shoulders and held her aloft. She looked up at him uncertainly. 'You don't want me to…?'

His dark eyes glittered with rampant desire. 'I want you to but not here and not now,' he said. 'You will come to me next Thursday. I will make sure we will not be disturbed. You can stay the night.'

She lowered her gaze. 'I can't stay the night…'

He brought up her chin with a determined finger. 'I will send a car for you.'

'You're not listening to me, Sebastian. I can't stay with you.'

'Why not?'

She bit her lip searching for a plausible excuse. 'I have to work the next day. I don't want to compromise my work situation. If I turn up late I could lose my job.'

'You will not lose your job,' he said. 'Besides, I have already requested your presence at the party I am holding for the children on the following Friday at the palace.'

Cassie's eyes rounded in alarm. 'The party is on Friday?' she asked. '*Next* Friday?'

'Yes,' he said. 'That was what Stefanos confirmed when he brought in our lunch. I wanted to do it sooner rather than later as with the coronation preparations my diary will not be so easy to juggle in the weeks to come. We are going ahead with it, otherwise it could be weeks or even months before I can see to it.'

Cassie was finding it hard to hold his gaze. She had to fight not to show how deeply disturbed she was by the news of the party. What if one of the staff mentioned to Sebastian she was Sam's mother? She could hardly tell Sophie and Kara and the others not to mention it, otherwise they might begin to suspect something. She would have to be so vigilant, keeping close to Sam the whole time. That was all she could do.

'I can't stay overnight,' Cassie repeated, chewing at her lip even more desperately. 'I will have to start work earlier on Friday to prepare the children for the party.'

'All right,' he said after a tense pause. 'I will agree to have you returned to your house after our date.'

Our date.

Cassie's mouth twisted at the euphemism. 'You've really changed, Sebastian. You never used to be so cold-bloodedly ruthless.'

'If you find me a little more ruthless than before you have only yourself to blame,' he countered. 'You did a good job on me, Cassandra Kyriakis. Whenever I become involved with a woman I take control at the start and I make sure I still have it at the finish.'

Cassie clenched her hands by her sides, her fingertips digging into her palms almost painfully. 'I'm not going to be your latest whore,' she said with a last stand of pride. 'I'd rather be locked up again for the next twenty years than suffer that fate.'

He had the gall to laugh. 'Oh, such feisty words, but do you have any idea of how foolish you are being?'

'It can't be any more foolish than agreeing to lie on my back for you to paw me whenever you like,' she shot back.

'Do you think I want it to be this way?' he asked as a flicker of anger lit his gaze from behind. 'I wish I could look at you and feel nothing, but that's not the way it is.'

'It's your pride,' she said. 'You want to rewrite the past because I…because…' she lowered her eyes from him '…I wasn't faithful to you.'

'It is not my pride,' he ground out harshly. 'I want you because I have never wanted anyone else like I want you.'

Cassie swallowed back her anguish at his grudging confession. She felt exactly the same way about him, but the secret of their son yawned like a deep, unbridgeable canyon between them. If he found out about Sam now Sebastian's whole life would change irreparably.

All she had to say was: *Five years ago I had your son.*

Cassie felt close to tears. She could feel them building at the back of her tight throat, their burning presence a stinging reminder of how much she had loved Sebastian, even though he had ignored her one point of contact with him via her letter, even though he had trashed her character all over again by offering her a short clandestine affair so similar to the one he had offered her six years ago.

'I really need to get going,' she said, fiddling with her watch.

He stepped closer and traced the pad of his index finger down the slope of her cheek. 'One week,' he said, locking gazes with her. 'Believe me, Cassie, I will not let this rest until I have one night with you.'

Cassie wished she had the strength and will power to say no. Any other person and it would have been so easy. But didn't she owe it to him? She'd had his son. She might not ever be in a position to inform him of it, but surely she owed him an hour or two of her time so she could one day tell Sam what sort of man his father was without revealing his true identity.

She had been lucky so far. Sam was surrounded by children

who had not just one parent, but *no* parents. It hadn't yet occurred to Sam to ask why he didn't have a father, but she knew in the years to come he would no doubt do so. She had no idea how she would handle the subject. Lying to her little boy seemed morally wrong, and yet wouldn't it be equally morally reprehensible to destroy Sebastian's lifelong goal of ruling his people by informing him he had a love-child?

'I guess if you want to see me on Thursday it could be arranged…' she said, feeling another piece of her heart curl up and die.

'I want to, *agape mou*,' Sebastian said, and brushed a soft kiss to her mouth. 'I want to very much.'

A knock sounded at the door and with a rueful expression he put her from him gently and strode over to answer it.

'Excuse me, Your Royal Highness,' Stefanos said. 'I wasn't sure if you were aware of the time. You have a meeting with the royal council in just less than fifteen minutes.'

'Thank you, Stefanos,' Sebastian said. 'You have timed it well. Dhespinis Kyriakis is just leaving. Could you ensure that she gets back to the orphanage safely?'

'Yes, indeed, Your Highness.'

Sebastian watched as Cassie picked up her purse and self-consciously straightened her clothes, her cheeks slightly pink and her eyes avoiding his as she brushed past.

'Until Thursday, Cassie,' he said so only she could hear it.

She stalled briefly, her fingers tightening on her purse, but then with a small, almost imperceptible nod she continued to move past him and followed the aide down the echoing corridor.

Sebastian puffed out his cheeks and let the breath escape in a long thin stream, his hand raking down his face in an effort to get his senses back into line. The last hour had been pure madness but it had proved one thing if nothing else.

What he had said to Cassie was right.

As stupid and misguided as it was, he was prepared to risk a very great deal to have her back in his arms, even if it was only for one night.

At the meeting a short time later Sebastian sat forwards in his chair, tapping his pen on the desk impatiently, his frown heavy. 'So there is still no sign of the Stefani diamond?' he asked his official council.

'I am afraid not, Your Highness,' the senior official answered soberly. 'The coronation plans are still in place but it makes things rather difficult.'

Sebastian had no time for someone stating the obvious. He knew what was at stake. The icon of the royal house of Karedes was the priceless Stefani diamond, the biggest of the rare pink diamonds found on the neighbouring island of Calista. The fact that the Anstan half had mysteriously disappeared was causing great mayhem in the royal household, for tradition had it no one could become King without the Stefani diamond in their coronation crown. King Zakari of Calista was already hunting for the Anstan half of the diamond, and if it was discovered he could unite both Aristo and Calista into the Kingdom of Adamas once more. This made it all the more imperative for Sebastian to solve the mystery and find the missing diamond.

'I want the investigation to continue until every person who ever handled the coronation crown is interviewed,' he instructed his officials. 'And of course there is no need to remind you of how this must remain within the palace walls. I do not want a press leak about this.'

Once the council meeting was over Sebastian called Stefanos aside. 'Two things, Stefanos, that I wish for you to see to immediately,' he said. 'Firstly, I would appreciate it if you would assist Demetrius in drawing up a guest list with each of the children's names on it and their carers. I would also like a small gift prepared for each child, appropriate for their age and gender. I will leave it in your very capable hands.'

'Yes, Your Highness.'

'Secondly, I would like you to make some enquiries for me,' Sebastian said, 'discreetly, of course.'

'But of course, Your Highness.'

'I want you to find out where Cassandra Kyriakis is living and if or when she was last involved with a lover,' Sebastian said with a determined set to his jaw.

'I will see to it immediately, Your Highness,' Stefanos said. 'Will that be all for now?'

Sebastian nodded as he clenched and unclenched his fingers inside his trouser pockets. 'For now,' he said, silently grinding his teeth.

After a quick word with Angelica, Cassie went into Sam's bedroom and sat on the edge of his bed, looking down at his innocent little face, so blissfully peaceful in sleep.

As she gently stroked the hair back off his forehead she thought of those first harrowing weeks in prison, how she had tried to adjust to being constantly under surveillance, not to mention the sleepless nights and terror-filled days. And that fateful day three months into her sentence when the prison doctor had called her down to the prison surgery for the results of the blood tests that had been ordered the week before. The news of her pregnancy had been an unbelievable shock. For several stunned days Cassie had been certain there must have been a mistake—a mix-up at the pathology laboratory or something. She couldn't possibly have been pregnant. She had been on the contraceptive pill since she was seventeen. She had not missed a period and apart from some breast tenderness and grumbling nausea and tiredness she had no other symptoms that could not have easily been put down to other causes. Stress, not eating, the death of her father…that last horrendous scene when he had tried to… Cassie had skittered away from memories, trying to keep a steady head in a world that had seemed intent on spinning out of her control, determined to find some other plausible reason why her body was so out of whack.

But in the end there had been no escaping it. The news of her pregnancy and the subsequent birth of Sam had thankfully—and in Cassie's opinion miraculously—never been leaked to the press. The prison authorities had made special dispensation for her to keep the baby with her until he was of nursery-school age, when he had been fostered out until her release.

At least Cassie had been able to get Sam back, which was not always the case with other women. She thought of the frayed photograph Angelica kept by her bedside of the dark-haired little boy, Nickolas, she had lost custody of during the height of her drug addiction. The boy's father had disappeared, taking Angelica's only reason for living with him. It had been four and a half years and Angelica still didn't know if her son was dead or alive.

Cassie bent forwards and softly kissed Sam's smooth brow. 'I am not going to let anyone take you away from me again,' she promised in a whisper. But the words seemed to echo faintly, as if fate had been listening on the sidelines and was already thinking of a way to step in once more.

CHAPTER SIX

'Your Royal Highness, I have that information you requested,' Stefanos said as he brought in Sebastian's coffee a couple of days later.

Sebastian lowered the newspaper he had been reading and gave his aide his full attention. 'What did you find out?'

'Cassandra Kyriakis is living at a small flat in Paros Lane with a former drug addict, a woman by the name of Angelica Mantoudakis. Apparently they met in prison but the Mantoudakis woman was released two years ago. She works at one of the local hotels as a housemaid.'

Sebastian's brows came together. 'What about a man?' he asked.

Stefanos shook his head. 'There is no man. However, there is a small child, a boy of about five or so.'

Sebastian straightened in his chair, a cold hand of unease disturbing the hairs on the back of his neck. 'A boy?' he asked, frowning harder. 'Who does he belong to?'

'I made some further enquiries and found out that Angelica Mantoudakis gave birth five years ago to a boy called Nickolas,' he said. 'I wasn't able to find out much else. The neighbours pretty much keep to themselves in that area, but one of them did say she sees Cassandra Kyriakis taking the little boy with her to the orphanage each day to the nursery school there, one assumes because the Mantoudakis woman's hours at the hotel prevent her doing so herself.'

Sebastian hadn't even realised he had been holding his breath until he let it out in a jagged stream of relief and something else he couldn't quite identify. 'Thank you, Stefanos,' he said. 'You did well.'

'The council have still not come up with any clues to the whereabouts of the Stefani diamond,' Stefanos went on. 'There is a private investigating team working on it, as well as Prince Alex, but so far nothing has come to light.'

Sebastian felt his jaw tighten all over again. He had lain awake half the night, wondering if the diamond would ever be found in time. No matter how discreet the private investigators would be he was under no illusions as to how long it would be before someone suspected something was amiss and rumours began to circulate. They had perhaps already begun to do so. Sebastian wanted the start of his rulership of Aristo to be as smooth as possible. He wanted to build the confidence of his people, to show them he was nothing like his autocratic father, but would listen to the various concerns brought to him from the community and act on them promptly and appropriately. He had a vision for Aristo, a vision he had nurtured from when he had first started to realise his destiny. He had been born to rule this island and he would do so with strong but considerate leadership, but unless the Stefani diamond was found, his coronation could not go ahead.

'Keep them on to it,' he instructed his aide. 'And make sure they keep their heads down while they are at it.'

'Certainly, Your Highness,' Stefanos said, and after a pause added, 'I have just been talking to Demetrius about the orphanage party. The director of the orphanage was delighted with the invitation as you are the first patron to have made such a magnanimous gesture.'

Sebastian waved away the compliment. 'They are children, Stefanos,' he said. 'Little defenceless children with no one to look out for them. It is the very least I can do.'

'Yes, indeed, Your Highness,' Stefanos agreed. 'So is the dinner with Cassandra Kyriakis going ahead for Thursday night? I will have to let the chef know.'

'It is going ahead,' Sebastian said, leaning back in his chair. 'I want to take her to Kionia for a picnic.'

Stefanos lifted his brows for a nanosecond. 'I will see to it immediately,' he said, and left.

Cassie was hovering near the window when the long, black, sleek car pulled up in front of the flat on Thursday evening. She scooped up her purse and light wrap and made her way outside even before the driver could get to the front door to ring the doorbell.

The uniformed driver opened the passenger door for her with a blank expression, and she slipped inside, coming face to face with Sebastian, who was sitting on the plush leather seat opposite hers.

'I can see you are in a hurry for our date, *agape mou*,' he observed with a benign smile. 'How flattering.'

Cassie rolled her eyes in disdain and shifted her knees so they weren't brushing against his. 'That's not the case at all,' she said with chilly hauteur. 'I didn't want to draw attention to myself or to you. Can you imagine what the neighbours would make of me going off in a limousine?'

'I take your point,' he said, still smiling. 'Would you like a drink? I would offer you champagne but you would not drink it, *ne?* But there is fresh orange juice or mineral water.'

'Orange juice would be lovely… Thank you.'

Once he had poured her a chilled glass of juice and handed it to her, Cassie settled back in her seat and tried to relax her shoulders. She took a covert look at him over the rim of her frosted glass as she took a small sip of her drink. He was wearing taupe-coloured trousers and a white open-neck shirt, the sleeves rolled up to almost his elbows giving him a handsome-without-really-trying look that was nothing short of heart-stopping. She felt her breath come to a skidding halt in her chest just looking at him. He was cleanly shaven, his curly black hair springy and damp from his recent shower. The citrus-based fragrance of his aftershave drifted towards her and she couldn't stop the flare of her nostrils to take more of the alluring scent in. How could a man so casually dressed be so overwhelmingly masculine? she wondered. The breadth of his shoulders, the taut flatness of his abdomen and the long muscular length of his thighs were an over-whelming reminder of his potency as a full-blooded man in the prime of his life.

'How was your day?' he asked.

Cassie lowered her glass with an unsteady hand. 'M-my day?'

His mouth tilted in a disarming manner that reminded her so much of Sam she felt her stomach muscles involuntarily tighten.

'Yes, Cassie, your day,' he said. 'Did you work at the or-phanage?'

'Yes…'

'How was Nickolas?'

Cassie looked at him blankly. 'Nickolas?'

He set his glass down on the flip-top rest at his elbow. 'Your flatmate's son,' he said. 'The one you take with you to the orphanage nursery-school each day.'

Cassie licked her suddenly arid-dry lips.

'Um…he's…he's…how…how did you find out…about him?'

'I had my aide Stefanos make some discreet enquiries about who you were living with.'

Cassie felt her heart pumping so erratically she was sure he would hear it, but she forced herself to hold his penetrating coal-black gaze in any case, even though every instinct inside was screaming for her to avoid it. 'So,' she said with an attempt at nonchalance she was sure had fallen well short of the mark, 'what else did you find out about me?'

He picked up his glass once more and twirled it in his hand in an indolent manner. 'Your flatmate is an ex-prisoner. A drug addict, apparently. Hardly the company you should be keeping if you are serious about turning your life around, now, is it?'

Her chin came up at that. 'I hope you're not going to hold her past against her,' she said. 'Angelica is one of the most genuine and loving people I have ever met. She deserves a second chance.'

'Is she clean?'

She set her mouth. 'Yes, she is.'

'She would want to be, given she's the mother of a small child,' he commented imperiously.

Cassie listened to her deafening heartbeats reverberating through her eardrums: *kaboom, kaboom, kaboom…*

So he assumed Sam was her flatmate's child, she thought with somewhat cautious relief. That was a good thing…for now. As long as she could maintain the charade with Angelica's cooperation for the next few weeks until she left the island for good things would be fine…or so Cassie hoped.

'Did you meet her in prison?' he asked.

'Yes.'

'So the child was with her in prison?'

'Um…' Cassie mentally crossed her fingers at yet another one of her little white lies. 'Yes…'

He gave her a studied look for a lengthy moment. 'The little boy whose drawing you gave me the other day,' he said. 'Did he come from a criminal or violent background?'

Cassie's hand trembled slightly as she reached for her glass of juice. 'Not directly…'

One of Sebastian's brows hooked upwards. 'Meaning what exactly?'

'His mother would never dream of being violent towards him.'

A frown appeared on his brow. 'But I thought you said he was an orphan?'

Cassie stared at him for a heart-stopping moment. 'Um… I…I…' she gave a tight little swallow '…did I?'

He gave a single nod. 'You did.'

'Oh…well, I must have got him confused with another child…or something…'

'What is his name?' he asked.

Cassie's heart gave another pounding thump. 'N-name?'

'The little boy who gave me the drawing,' he said. 'What is his name?'

She ran her tongue across her lips. 'It's…er…Sam.'

'I am looking forward to meeting him tomorrow at the party,' Sebastian said. 'I have organised a magician to entertain them as well as a gift for every child and the mandatory balloons, sweets, cakes and ices.'

'That's very generous of you,' Cassie said, her heart still pounding sickeningly. She could even feel a fine trail of perspiration making its way between her shoulder blades. 'I'm sure they will have a wonderful time and remember it for the rest of their lives.'

'I would like to make it an annual event,' he said. 'And I would like to visit the orphanage as soon as it can be arranged.'

'I am sure the director will be delighted to have you do so,' Cassie said, even as her heart gave another gut-wrenching lurch of dread. The party at the palace was risky enough, but if Sebastian wandered around the orphanage on an official visit someone was surely going to inadvertently let the cat out of the bag over who Sam's mother was. Cassie had already told so many fibs. It was getting harder and harder to keep each brick of untruth in place. Any minute she felt as if the wall of lies she had built would tumble down and crush her. Even the way Sebastian looked at her in that unwavering way of his made her wonder if he suspected something was amiss. At times she felt as if it were written in block letters on her forehead: *I am the mother of your little son.* All Sebastian had to do was keep looking at her in that piercing way of his and he would surely see it.

Just the way he was looking at her now…

'Have you guessed where I am taking you?' he asked after a few moments of silence.

Cassie leaned forward to look out of the window. They had moved well beyond the town and were heading to the Bay of Kounimai where she knew the Karedes family had a private holiday retreat at a place called Kionia. Sebastian had never taken her there before but in the past he had told her of the secluded beauty of the villa with its fabulous views over the rough water of the passage separating Aristo from the neighbouring island of Calista. 'Are we going to Kionia?' she asked as she sat back in her seat.

'Yes,' he said. 'I thought we could both do with some privacy.

I had Stefanos organise a picnic for us. It is a pleasant evening with not too much sea breeze so we can enjoy the sunset.'

'It sounds lovely,' Cassie said. 'I can't remember the last time I went on a picnic. Sam's always asking me to—' She suddenly stopped, her heart thudding like an out-of-sync timepiece.

Sebastian cocked his head at her. 'Sam? You mean the little boy who drew me the picture?'

Cassie blinked at him, her brain whirling and spinning out of control. 'Um…he's…Angelica's little boy,' she finally managed to croak out.

He gave her a quizzical look. 'I thought his name was Nickolas,' he said. 'Or at least that's what Stefanos said it was, but then he could have got it wrong.'

'N-no, that is right…' Cassie hastily mortared another lie into her wall of deceit. 'Angelica's son is called Nickolas but…but he prefers his second name…'

'Like my sister prefers Lissa or Liss instead of Elissa,' he said.

Cassie felt her tension gradually start to dissipate, but even so her stomach felt as if a hive of bees had taken up residence inside. She felt as if each wing were buzzing against the lining of her stomach, the threat of a thousand stings making the trail of perspiration along her backbone feel more like a river. 'Yes…exactly like that…'

'I told her I ran into you,' Sebastian said. 'She's been in Paris studying. She came home for our father's funeral and Kitty's wedding, but now she's in Australia working for a friend of Alex's, a businessman by the name of James Black.'

'How is she?' Cassie asked, thinking with more than a pang or two of shame of the wild-child antics Lissa and she had got up to. It was hard to remember now who had encouraged whom, but Cassie suspected she was the one who had been held most responsible.

'You know Lissa,' he said with a rueful twist to his mouth.

'If there's a party she not only wants to be there but she wants to be the centre of it. She wasn't too keen about being packed off to Sydney but we all thought it best if she had some time in the real world. I just hope it irons out some of her wilfulness. She has always been a little too independent for her own good.'

Cassie looked down at her hands for a moment. 'I am sure the experience of travelling and working abroad will be wonderful for her. When you are next speaking to her…I mean, if you think it's appropriate to mention you have seen me, please tell her I send my regards.'

The car growled its way into the wrought iron fortress of the Karedeses' private hideaway, making the silence inside all the more intense. Cassie felt the press of Sebastian's watchful gaze and forced herself to bring her eyes back to his.

'No doubt she will contact you in due course,' he said, still with his dark, penetrating gaze trained on her face. 'When my father found out about the postcards she sent he strictly forbade any further contact while he was alive, which I think Lissa feels guilty about now. That is probably why she hasn't as yet contacted you.'

'I understand,' she said. 'We were probably not a good mix when I think about it. We brought out the worst in each other at times.'

'She was always very fond of you.'

Cassie felt her heart contract. 'I was…I *am* still very fond of her,' she said, and then unguardedly added, 'We had more in common than she probably realised.'

He gave her one of his narrow-eyed looks. 'What do you mean?'

Her gaze skittered away from his. 'The children of high-profile parents often have a lot in common. We are constantly followed by the press and anything we do or say is used against us. I think Lissa and I were alike in that we got fed up with it all and tried to get out there and live like other normal teenagers. But of course we could never be normal, Lissa more so than me. She, like you, has royal blood running through her veins.'

'You are right, of course,' he said. 'I too had to pull in my horns, so to speak. The weight of responsibility does that to you after a while. Even if my father had not died so unexpectedly I was already feeling the urge to settle down.'

Cassie felt a pain like a rusty switchblade go through her. Sebastian had already mentioned a suitable wife had been selected for him. She could see him married to a beautiful woman who was everything she was not nor ever could be: gracious, well-bred, with an immaculate reputation, well educated and comfortable in every social situation. No doubt his wonderfully suitable wife would bear him an heir and a spare, maybe even another couple of gorgeous children who looked just like Sam…

Even if she was thousands of kilometres away as she had planned, how on earth would Cassie bear it?

Sebastian instructed the driver to set up the picnic in a secluded spot near some tamarisk trees that provided a shelter of sorts a short distance from the stately royal holiday residence.

Within minutes a table with crisp white linen was set up, sparkling crystal glasses and crested silverware set out in preparation for a meal fit for…well, royalty of course, Cassie thought wryly as she watched a solid silver vase complete with red rose being placed in the very centre of the table. It was certainly nothing like the picnics Cassie had been on in the past, with floppy paper plates, plastic forks and knives that wouldn't cut through melted butter let alone anything else.

The food provided by the royal kitchen was nothing short of delightful, every morsel was a work of art in itself, and artfully arranged to entice even the most jaded of appetites.

Sebastian led Cassie to the silky fabric-covered chair opposite his, and, once he was sure she was comfortable, took his own seat, instructing the driver-cum-waiter to serve their meal.

Cassie had not felt in the least bit hungry, but as soon as the tiny dishes appeared in front of her she found herself partaking of a feast that was beyond belief. Char-grilled octopus, garlic mussels, plump prawns skewered on tiny sticks with a lime and coriander marinade, ripe olives and semi sun-dried tomatoes, followed by pesto-encrusted succulent grilled chicken with a variety of lightly steamed vegetables, and to top it off a vanilla bean crème caramel custard with plump summer berries.

Cassie had declined all alcohol, but the absence of fine wine had not for a moment taken away from the delectable feast she had partaken of. With her stomach replete and her taste buds still zinging with the fresh and fantastic flavours she had consumed, she felt as if she had been transported into another realm. After years of stolid prison food served haphazardly by other inmates, with the nagging suspicion of someone tampering with the meal as a payback for supposed misdemeanours, Cassie had not realised how much she had missed out on until now.

Did Sebastian have any idea of what he took for granted every single day? Meals were put in front of him morning, noon and night, nutritious, gourmet and delectable meals prepared by world-renowned chefs. He had never had to bargain or bribe to get a mouthful of food for himself, nor had he ever had to beg, borrow or steal to provide a tiny treat for his little son.

Sebastian poured himself a small measure of red wine, watching the fleeting emotions passing over Cassie's face. She had been very quiet during the meal. He had watched as she had taken tiny bites of each morsel with her small white teeth, her eyes lighting up as she savoured each mouthful, chewing slowly, as if wanting the flavours to last as long as possible. She used her cutlery with the grace and elegance of someone brought up with a refined sense of dining. He had met and dated women who had spent a year in a finishing school who had less class and poise than Cassie, which was a credit to her father, he supposed, given Cassie's mother had not been around.

'Was it lonely for you growing up without a mother?' Sebastian asked, hardly realising the question had fallen from his lips until the sea-washed silence was broken by it.

Her eyes moved upwards to meet his, a shadow of something dark and mysterious lurking in their startling emerald depths. 'I'm not sure it is possible to miss something you have never had,' she said in an offhand tone that didn't quite do the job of convincing Sebastian she meant it. 'I had a series of nannies who looked after me when my father was at work. I had toys and entertainment, more than most kids have, or at least certainly more than the kids I deal with now.'

Sebastian surveyed her features as he cradled his wineglass in his hand. 'You didn't answer my question, Cassie,' he said.

Cassie shifted her eyes from his and inwardly frowned. Why was he doing this? In the past he had hardly ever asked her about her life as a child. They hadn't had that sort of relationship. Their love affair—strike that—sex affair—had had nothing to do with getting to know each other as people. It had been lust that had driven them into each other's arms, a forbidden lust that had made it all the more exciting. Cassie's body quivered as she thought of the things they had done and where they had done them. The thrill of being discovered had been part of the adrenalin rush.

Cassie shifted in her chair, her face averted from the all-seeing gaze of Sebastian's. 'I guess it would have been nice to have had a mother...especially during adolescence,' she said, absently fiddling with the edge of the tablecloth. 'I try not to think about it too much. Lots of people don't have mothers and survive. I am hardly unique.'

'No, that is true, but you have never really talked about what it was like for you as a child,' he said. 'I guess I should have been more mature back when we were involved and asked you. But then like a lot of young men with hormones on their mind I didn't get around to it.'

Cassie wasn't brave enough to meet his eyes. She knew in any case what she would see there: desire, hot and strong, perhaps even stronger than what he had felt for her before. What she couldn't understand was why. She was the last person he should be considering associating with. She had a black mark on her name that would never go away, no matter how far away from Aristo she travelled. Her life was never going to be the same again. Not that it had been all that crash-hot to start with.

Cassie had spent years of her early childhood desperately trying to please her father to no avail. She couldn't quite recall how old she had been when she had changed her tactics and begun to rebel against him instead. All she could remember were the fights, the vicious slanging matches that had nearly always ended with her being—

'Cassie…' Sebastian's deep voice jerked her out of her torturous memories.

Cassie blinked at him, trying to recall what they had been talking about, her mind still back in her bedroom with her father's puce features glaring at her, his mouth a tight white line of livid rage, spittle pooling at the corners, his teeth audibly grinding together as his closed thick fist had raised, ready to strike…

She swallowed a painfully tight swallow that tore at the tender lining of her throat, her eyes skittering away from Sebastian's. Nausea roiled in her stomach, her blood pressure dropped so low she could feel the sensation of fine grains of sand shifting in her extremities. She was going to faint... No...hang on a minute...she was holding on...but only just... Breathe...deep and even, that was the way to do it. It had been years since she'd had a panic attack. She knew the drill; it just took a little discipline and focus to pull it off.

Breathe...in...out...in...out...in—

'Caz?' Sebastian leaned forward across the table and took her ice-cold hand in his, his brow furrowed in concern. 'What's going on? You've gone as white as a sheet. What is wrong?'

Cassie forced her lips into a smile but it made her face feel strangely disconnected from her mind. 'Nothing,' she said in what she hoped sounded like an offhand manner. 'I forgot what we were talking about. I was thinking about something else.'

He was still frowning at her. 'Whatever you were thinking about must have been distressing for you,' he said. 'Was it something to do with your time in prison?'

Cassie sat back in her chair and crossed her legs. She was as close to crumbling as she had ever been, but some tiny rod of pride kept her spine upright. 'You seem to be rather fascinated with my prison life,' she speculated. 'Is that because you harbour some sort of fantasy about an ex-criminal? Sex with someone from the slammer. It has a sort of ring to it, don't you think?'

Sebastian felt his desire for her rise in his body with the force of an earthquake. It rumbled through him, it shook him, and above everything else—it challenged him.

He would have her.

It didn't matter how far apart their worlds were now. He would have her again to assuage this achingly tight need in his body that refused to go away. After all, wasn't that the way she had played it with him in the past? She had teased him, led him on and on until he had been out of his mind with lust.

It had all been a game to her, but he was going to play it by his own rules this time around, not hers.

Sebastian knew how her mind worked. She was as good as penniless now. Sure, she seemingly enjoyed working at the orphanage, but the Cassie Kyriakis he had known six years ago would have turned her nose up at such menial, poorly paid work. He just couldn't imagine her soothing sobbing infants or wiping dripping noses, much less changing dirty nappies. He even remembered her telling him at one point how she never wanted to have children, that she intended to spend her life constantly partying, making the most of the wealth her father had accumulated.

Sebastian hadn't let it bother him too much at the time; he had dated plenty of rich young women with exactly the same mindset. And he had been well aware of his royal duty when the time came to find an impeccable wife who would willingly bear his royal heirs. Not for a moment had he thought Cassie Kyriakis a likely candidate…and yet…

Sebastian gave himself a stern mental shake. So what if his physical relationship with Cassie had for all these years since been unsurpassed? That did not necessarily mean there was no other woman out there who could not meet his needs in the same way or better. Anyway, it was only the deluded romantic fools of the world who claimed there was only one perfect soul mate for each person.

What utter nonsense!

Sebastian would show how misguided such a philosophy could be. He was even prepared to bet he would be disappointed in a repeat performance with Cassie. Memories did that to you. They glorified the past until the real thing was often a let-down, making you wonder why you had craved it so assiduously in the first place.

God knew how many men she had opened her legs for

since him. It coiled his gut with writhing, vicious vipers of jealousy to think of the men she had been with during the time they had been secretly conducting their affair. How could he know how many men she had given herself to?

Yes, it was perhaps sexist of him to judge her by different standards from his own, but she had *lied* to him, damn it! She had told him making love with him was the most amazing, out-of-this-world experience, and fool that he was he had believed her. How many other men had she gazed up at with those shining emerald eyes of hers, her lips swollen with passion, and said the very same thing?

'Would you like some more water?' Sebastian asked with no hint of what he had been thinking evident in his polite, solicitous tone.

'No…thank you…' Cassie said, placing her napkin down on the table. 'The meal was delicious. Thank you for going to so much trouble. It has certainly raised the bar on any future picnics I might have in the future.'

'It was nothing,' he said with a wry smile. 'I didn't lift a finger. I wouldn't know how to make a canapé if you paid me.'

There was a stretched-out silence with only the raging sea below to break it. *Boom…crash…boom…crash…*

'What about coffee?' Sebastian asked over the suddenly deafening sound of the waves against the shore. 'Stefanos has arranged coffee and chocolates inside. I wanted to make the most of the sunset but the breeze has stiffened now the sun has gone down. You have goose bumps—would you like my jacket?'

Cassie didn't like to tell him the pinpricks on her skin were from apprehension rather than cold, even though, as he had said, the breeze from the rough water below had only recently picked up its pace. She could see the galloping white horses of the waves, each one racing to crash against the shore in a foamy, almost angry wash against the rocks and sand. But before she could refuse the offer of his jacket he was on his feet and behind her chair, covering her shoulders in the warm citrus-scented folds of his coat.

Cassie felt as if she had just stepped into his skin, so intimate was the gesture, the light but firm touch of his hands on her shoulders as he set the jacket in place rendering her speechless with longing for more of his touch. She breathed in the spicy fragrance, all of her senses suddenly hyper-vigilant, and her heart in very great danger of making the same mistake it had made six years before.

Sebastian escorted her on the short trip to the private royal residence, a massive villa with views from every vantage point. Stefanos was nowhere in sight, but Cassie assumed he had been given instructions to make himself scarce. She couldn't help wondering with a jab of pain how many other times he had been issued with the same orders while Sebastian entertained other women.

As if Sebastian had read her thoughts, he said as he led the way into the opulent foyer, 'I think you should know at this point you are the very first person I have brought here. This is the private holiday residence for my family, off limits to everyone except only close family and closely trusted friends.'

Cassie raised her brows at him as he closed the heavy door behind him. 'So, Sebastian,' she said. 'Which category do I fall into? Surely you do not consider me a close friend or a future member of the royal family?'

Tension travelled all the way from his darker-than-dark eyes to his chiselled jaw and then to his thinned-out mouth. 'Given our history, Cassie, you are not eligible for either of those positions,' he bit out tightly.

Cassie wished with all her heart she could reveal Sam's identity and throw the truth of their situation in his face to make him realise how much she was a part of his wretched royal family whether he liked it or not, but some remnant of self-respect and self-preservation prevented her from doing so. Instead she smiled up at him, a cool, calculating smile that gave him no clue to the turmoil going on inside her. 'I consider myself deeply honoured, Your Royal Highness,' she drawled with a bow of her head that deliberately fell short of the mark, delivering the insult she had intended. 'It is indeed a privilege to be considered worthy of gracing the highly esteemed private residence of the Karedes family, considering the lower than low background I come from.'

'Your background was nothing to be ashamed of until you took it upon yourself to degrade your father at every opportunity,' he said. 'His public role was made a hundred times worse by the way you behaved.'

Twenty-four years of Cassie's suffering threatened to come to the surface, like a volcano silently brewing until the temperature of the lava became too hot to contain. A catastrophic explosion was imminent, but somehow she was able to contain the emotion she felt to remind herself no one knew her father as she had known him. No one had heard the soul-destroying words he had flung at her in one of his many out-of-control tempers; no one had seen the bruises his hands, not to mention any other objects within his reach, had left on her body.

Sebastian had not seen the jagged scar low on her back her father had scored into her flesh that fateful day. It was like a tattoo of torment, the brand her father had left to remind her of how he had demanded total control of her, a control she had not given willingly and had fought every inch of the way as each strike of his belt had bitten cruelly and cuttingly into her flesh.

Cassie had been so proud that she hadn't cried. She had gritted her teeth until she was sure they would crack under the pressure. She had taken every vicious cut of the strap like a convict bracing for the cat-o'-nine-tails.

That had been her victory.

Her father could blame her for her mother's untimely death, he could blame her for having been a small, needy and insecure child, and he could even blame her for being an out-of-control, wilful teenager, but he could not blame her for reclaiming her life and that of her child. That had been her only solace. Her father had not known of Sam's existence. Her tiny precious son had been even to Cassie, unknown in her womb at the time of that dreadful scene. Whether her father would have acted differently if he had known she was carrying a royal baby was something she would never know.

But Cassie knew she had choices now and one was to keep a cool head. Sebastian's presence admittedly made that task difficult, but she had to keep a lid on her emotions, at all times and in all places.

She *had* to.

Cassie lifted her gaze to his, her spine not quite so rigid, her shoulders going down beneath the sheltering warmth of his jacket. 'My father was not a good father,' she said. 'He might have been a brilliant mayor and an astute businessman, but he didn't love and protect me the way he should have done. You didn't know him personally, Sebastian. You knew of him from what your father and other palace officials told you.' Her eyes misted over suddenly as she added in a choked up voice, 'But you didn't *know* him.'

Sebastian let out a rusty sigh and, taking one single step, gathered her to him. He rested his chin on the top of her head and wondered why the hell he still felt this way about her. She could go from a shrieking shrew to a lost little girl within a heartbeat. Then, to make things even more confusing, she could turn on the heat and turn into a sensual goddess, that pouting mouth of hers making him want to press his down on those blood-red lips and never stop kissing her, devouring her taste, the essence of her body, .o feel the convulsions of her feminine muscles around him, making him pour himself into her. He could feel the movement of his blood in his veins; he was already hard against her and wondered why she hadn't moved back.

He felt her take in a breath, the brush of her breasts against his chest making him shudder with the need to fill her as he had done in the past.

He lifted her chin and looked into the sea-glass-green of her eyes, fighting not to drown in them. 'You are right,' he said. 'I didn't know him personally. He seemed very affable but I know from personal experience that what goes on in public is not always representative of what happens in private.'

She looked back at him, her gaze as unfathomable as the ocean pounding below. 'I'm cold,' she said and he felt her shiver under the touch of his hands.

Sebastian took one of her hands from where it was clutching at his jacket to keep it in place, and brought it up to his mouth. He kissed each of her knuckles in turn, a soft-as-a-baby's sigh caress that made her pupils grow darker than the sea raging below. 'Then let's go inside and warm you up,' he said, and, taking her by the hand, he led her inside the villa.

CHAPTER SEVEN

CASSIE stepped into the private study Sebastian opened a short time later, her senses heightened by his light touch as he took his jacket from her shoulders and laid it over a chair.

He came back to stand in front of her, his dark gaze meshing with hers as he took both of her hands in his. 'Not so cold now?' he asked.

She shook her head, her tongue darting out to moisten her lips. 'No...not cold at all...'

He settled his hands on her waist and brought her up against his body. 'I should pour you a cup of coffee,' he said, looking down at her mouth.

Cassie felt her lips start to tingle the longer his gaze rested there. 'Should you?' she asked.

He smiled lopsidedly. 'You do not fancy a coffee right now, *agape mou?*'

Cassie drew in a shaky breath, her stomach feeling hollow with a combination of nerves and anticipation. 'That's not really why I am here, is it, Sebastian?'

He placed his palm at the nape of her neck, his fingers warm and tempting on her sensitive skin. 'You still want to deny what is between us, Cassie?' he asked.

How could she possibly deny it? Cassie wondered. What

would be the point? Saying no to Sebastian Karedes had never been easy for her, now even more so. They both knew she was here because she wanted to be here. By stepping over the threshold of the villa she had stepped into his arms and would stay there for as long as he wanted her to. 'No,' she said, placing her hands on his chest as she met his gaze. 'I am not going to deny it.'

He brought his mouth down to hers in a slow-moving assault on her senses, waiting until she opened her mouth on a whimpering sigh before he began to stroke her tongue with his own. The erotic caress loosened her spine, her legs swaying beneath her as he deepened the kiss, each slow thrust and stroke of his tongue fuelling her desire until all she could think about was how it would feel to have him possess her again.

His kiss changed its tempo as soon as her hands pulled his shirt out of his trousers, his mouth grinding against hers. Tongues of flame licked along her veins as she responded by rubbing up against him, her hands going to his waistband, unbuckling him and uncovering him with her searching fingers.

Cassie swallowed his gasp of reaction as her fingers danced along his length, the satin strength of him so potently male, so aroused he was seeping with moisture. She played with him, squeezing, rubbing and stroking him while her mouth was being plundered by his, her heart rate soaring, her body slick and wet with need.

He muttered something unintelligible as he tore his mouth off hers, his dark eyes glittering with pent-up desire, his hands already lifting her skirt, his clever, artful fingers searching for the secret heart of her desire, behind the thin lace of her knickers.

She quivered against his touch, the smooth stroking of his fingers, curling her toes and arching her back until she was gasping out loud, the shock waves of release reverberating through her.

The ripples of reaction were still rolling through her as he backed her to the nearest wall, only stopping long enough to retrieve a condom from his jacket pocket on the way past.

Cassie shivered in delight as she helped him sheath himself, the urgency in his movements building her desire all over again.

She shuddered as he surged into her moist warmth, his thickness stretching her, sending wave after wave of rapture through her with each deep, pounding thrust.

He set a furiously fast rhythm, as if he were riding against an approaching storm, each rocking movement of his body in hers bringing him closer and closer to the point of no return. She felt it building in his body, the increasing tautness of his muscles, the sucking in of his breath, the contortion of his features as he hovered for that infinitesimal moment, before exploding his need inside her, each last thrust accompanied by a primal grunt of deep male satisfaction.

Cassie listened to his breathing as he held her against him in the quiet glow of the aftermath, wondering how she had lived without the magic of his touch for so long. Her body felt tender and swollen from his almost rough possession, but she would not have admitted it for the world. Let him think she was used to a quick tumble wherever she could get it. It would make their inevitable parting neater and cleaner, for him at least. It would never be anything other than heartbreakingly painful for her.

A chirruping sound broke through her reverie but it was a moment or two before she realised what it was. Her small purse containing her mobile was sitting on the chair where Sebastian's jacket was draped.

'Is that your phone?' he asked, easing away from her.

Cassie straightened her clothes. 'Um, yes...but it was just someone leaving a message.'

He frowned as he glanced at his watch. 'Who would be texting you at this time of night?' he asked.

Cassie hoped her expression was not revealing anything of the rapid pulse of panic she could feel in her chest. 'It's probably my flatmate, Angelica. She is no doubt wondering where I am.'

He was still frowning slightly. 'Did you tell her who you were with?'

'Of course not,' she said, dropping her gaze.

Sebastian lifted her chin between his thumb and index finger. 'Word must not get out about our assignation, Cassie,' he said. 'I hope I can still trust you on that.'

She met his gaze with a flash of resentment in hers. 'Do you really think I would announce to all and sundry I have been chosen to service the future King of Aristo wherever and whenever he pleases?' she asked.

Sebastian set his mouth in a tight line. 'You were with me all the way, Cassie.'

She tugged his hand away from her face. 'I want to go home.'

'Not yet,' he said. 'I haven't finished with you.'

She glared at him but he could see the up-and-down movement of her throat as her eyes darted to her purse again.

'Aren't you going to read the message?' he asked, pinning her with his gaze.

The point of her tongue swept over her lips. 'I'm sure it's nothing important…'

Sebastian moved over to the chair and, scooping up her purse, came back and handed it to her. 'Why don't you check it to make sure?'

She hesitated just long enough for his suspicion of her to be heightened. She was hiding something; he was sure of it now. Perhaps she had a lover in spite of what Stefanos's covert enquiries had uncovered. He felt his insides twisting with jealousy; he would *not* share her.

He watched as she opened the face of her phone, her fingers fumbling as she pressed the text-message-viewing button. Her eyes widened for a moment, before she gathered herself, her face becoming an expressionless mask as she closed the phone and slipped it back into her purse.

'Nothing urgent?' he asked, watching her closely.

'My flatmate is feeling unwell,' she said. 'I think I should go back now to make sure she is all right.'

Sebastian knew she was lying. He could feel it. Damn it, he could see it in her eyes, the way they couldn't quite hold his. But he had plenty of time to uncover her deceit. He had offered her an affair and as far as he was concerned it had started tonight and would continue for as long as he wanted. What they had shared had been a foretaste of the pleasure he would take from her until he was satisfied she would rue the day she had walked away from him and into the arms of another man.

'I will summon Stefanos to bring the car around,' he said and, striding over to the desk, pressed a button on an intercom system.

Cassie sat in the limousine beside Sebastian a few minutes later, her features schooled into indifference. Angelica had sent her the message that Sam had woken with a bad dream and had refused to go back to bed until his mother came home.

As the car got closer she felt her panic building. What if Sam heard the car pulling up and opened the front door? Or what if he had worked himself up into hysteria by now and could be heard from the street?

The car purred to a halt outside the flat, which, after the opulent luxury of the royal hideaway, looked even shabbier and more run-down.

'Are you going to ask me in for coffee?' Sebastian asked as he helped Cassie from the car.

Cassie swallowed and pulled her hand out of his, clutching her purse against her. 'It's late,' she said. 'I don't want to disturb Angelica.'

He stood watching her for a beat or two. 'Tell your flatmate I hope she makes a speedy recovery,' he said with an unreadable half-smile playing about his lips.

'I—I will,' she said and, turning, walked the short distance to the front door, the twin drills of his dark gaze boring holes into her back.

Cassie slipped inside the flat, closing the door behind her just as Angelica appeared in the narrow hallway. 'Is he all right?' she asked.

Angelica nodded. 'He went back to sleep almost as soon as I pressed Send on my phone. I hope I didn't interrupt anything important?'

Cassie shifted her gaze. She would tell Angelica everything at some point, but not now. 'No,' she said heading towards Sam's room. 'Nothing important…'

The children from the orphanage were excited for most of the following day about the party that afternoon. Cassie and her co-workers Sophie and Kara had a difficult time settling the smaller ones for their afternoon naps and even some of the older children had been unusually disruptive. Sam, on the other hand, was quiet and obedient.

Too quiet, Cassie thought with a pang of guilt. Had his nightmare last night been a result of her increasing unease over the past week? He was such a sensitive and intuitive child. He had wet the bed during the early hours of the morning, the first time in weeks, and he had been so ashamed he had tried to hide the evidence by spreading a towel over the sheets when she had come in. She had taken him in her arms and told him it was perfectly normal for accidents to happen and he wasn't to blame himself, but somehow she didn't think her reassurances had worked.

Cassie watched him as he stood in line to get on the bus the palace had sent for them. He had a frown of concentration between his small brows, making him look more like Sebastian than ever. Her insides twisted at the thought of them meeting face to face. Would Sebastian see something no one else had so far seen? she wondered. She scanned the two lines of children; so many of them had dark hair and dark eyes just like Sam. Her little son wouldn't stand out…she hoped.

The children quietened with awe as they were led inside the palace a few minutes later, the shuffle of their feet and the rustle of their clothes the only sound as they filed into one of the reception rooms which had been superbly decorated. Balloons hung in colourful clusters from the ceiling, the long ribbons attached making it easy for each child to reach to claim one once the party was over. The tables were loaded with party delights, fairy cakes, ice cream, chocolate and other treats that had every child bug-eyed with anticipation.

The Prince Regent was announced by one of the officials and Cassie held her breath as Sebastian came into the room. His gaze briefly met hers before he turned his attention to the children, who had been instructed to stand on his entry. She watched as he made a concentrated effort to put his young guests at ease. He soon dispensed with formality and moved from table to table, crouching down and chatting easily with each child as he gave them each a gift from the large bag his aide was carrying.

Cassie swallowed as Sebastian drew closer and closer to Sam. It seemed so obvious now they were in the same room together. The likeness was remarkable, startling…terrifying.

She hovered in the background, catching Sam's eye at one point and giving him an encouraging smile even as her insides churned.

'Hello, what is your name?' Sebastian said as he came to the child next to Sam.

'I'm Alexis,' the eight-year-old girl said with her usual precocity. 'And this is Sam. I'll open his present for him. He probably won't talk to you though, 'cause he's shy. He still wets his pants sometimes.'

Cassie felt her heart contract at Alexis's unthinking cruelty. Sam's cheeks were stained with colour and his dark brown gaze dropped in shame.

'Hello, Sam,' Sebastian said. 'I have been looking forward to meeting you.'

Sam's little head came up. 'Y-you have?' he asked in a whisper.

Sebastian's smile was easy and warm. 'Yes, it seems we have something in common,' he said. 'We both love to draw. I loved the painting you sent me. I have it in my study on my desk.'

A shy smile tugged at Sam's little mouth.

'You are much better than I was at your age' Sebastian said, still smiling, 'and you are not as shy as I was back then. I used to dread meeting people but after a while I got used to it. I am sure you will too.'

Cassie felt like hugging Sebastian; he couldn't have said anything better to put her son at ease. Sam was beaming up at him, his earlier shame all but forgotten.

She waited for Sebastian to move on, but he spent far longer with Sam than any other child. She held her breath for so long she saw a school of silverfish appear before her eyes. She blinked them away and forced herself to take a couple of calming breaths, but it wasn't until Sebastian moved on that she felt her shoulders come down in temporary relief.

Sebastian worked his way through the tables until every child had exchanged a few words with him, the sound of happy laughter and presents being unwrapped filling the room with joy.

Cassie had done her best to avoid him, but she could see, now that the magician had begun his act, Sebastian had been stealthily making his way to where she stood at the back of the room. She pressed herself back against the wall, wishing she could become as invisible as the rabbit the magician had made vanish just moments before.

'He is very good, is he not?' Sebastian said, indicating the magician, who was now pulling a long scarf out of one of the children's ears.

Her eyes moved away from his. 'Yes…he is…'

'The children are delightful,' he said after a moment. 'I'm so glad this afternoon has been a success.'

'Yes…you've made it very special for them and at such short notice. You must have very efficient staff.'

'I hope it wasn't too short for them,' he said, turning to look back at Sam's table with a small frown settling between his brows. 'When I was a little child it was often the anticipation of a special event that was the best part.'

The silence stretched for several heart-chugging seconds.

'I want to see you again tonight, Cassie,' Sebastian said, turning to face her.

Her eyes darted away from his. 'Um…I can't see you tonight…something's come up. I'm sure you understand how—'

'I understand one thing, Cassie, and that is I want to continue our association,' he said with an intransigent look. 'For the time being at least.'

She moistened her lips with the point of her tongue, her gaze flicking to where the children were seated, staring up at the magician as if he had cast a spell on them.

Sebastian took her arm and led her out of sight of the

tables. 'Listen to me, Cassie,' he demanded softly but no less implacably. 'This time I am the one who will say when our affair is over.'

She clawed at his hand around her wrist, her eyes shooting sparks of defiance at him. 'It's too dangerous,' she said. 'Can't you see that? Last night was a mistake. We should not have been together. It's over, Sebastian. It was over a long time ago.'

'Mummy?' A small child's voice sounded from behind Sebastian.

A gnarled hand clutched at his insides.

Mummy?

Sebastian turned and looked down at the little dark-haired boy called Sam who was chewing on his lip as he looked up at Cassie.

'Mummy, I need to go to the toilet but I don't know where it is. Can you take me?'

Sebastian felt a cold sensation go down his spine, like slow-moving ice. He swung his gaze back to Cassie. '*You* are Sam's mother?' he asked in a voice that sounded nothing like his.

Her face was shell-white, her eyes darting about in nervousness. 'I—I was going to tell you…' she began.

He frowned at her darkly, his thoughts shooting all over the place. God, she'd had a child. Somehow that hurt more than it should have. How had she kept such a thing a secret? He had heard no mention of a child. Why had she told him the boy was her flatmate's child? Why had she kept such a thing a…

He looked at the small boy again, his chest suddenly feeling as if something large and heavy had just backed over it and squeezed every scrap of air out of his lungs. He couldn't breathe. He couldn't speak. He stood frozen, every drop of blood in his body coming to a screaming, screeching halt.

Cassie had had a child while she was in prison, a child who

looked just like Sebastian. Thick, curly, black hair, dark brown eyes, olive skin and lean to the point of thin.

He had a son.

He had a child who had been kept a secret from him until now. Five years had passed and he had been robbed of every minute of his son's life. How many milestones had he missed? It tore at his insides to even think about them. When had he taken his first step? When had he said his first word? For God's sake, he didn't even know what day he had been born! Five birthdays had passed and he had not been there to celebrate any of them.

'Sorry, M-mummy,' Sam said with a wobble in his voice as he looked between them with eyes wide with worry. 'I tried to hold on but I had two glasses of lemonade. Will I get in trouble?'

'No…no, of course not, darling,' Cassie said, enveloping the boy in a hug. 'You're not in trouble at all. You're allowed to have all the lemonade you want.'

Sebastian watched as she slowly straightened, her eyes finally meeting his. He had thought he had hated her for what she had done to him before, but this was far worse. She had kept his son a secret, he could only assume deliberately. His mind began to reel at the thought of why she had left it this late. Had she planned to bring down the house of Karedes with a carefully timed press release?

He looked back down at Sam, the likeness hitting him over the head like a sledgehammer.

His son.

His son.

The words were running continuously in his head, like a recording stuck on one track.

He dragged his gaze back to Cassie's. 'We need to talk,' he somehow managed to get out past the thick, tight feeling in his throat.

Her eyes fell away. 'Not here…' She held the child close against her protectively. 'Not now.'

He clenched and unclenched his fists as he tried to keep control as she led Sam away. His insides were twisting as if a giant set of claws were attacking him. He felt a pain so intense he had to do everything in his power to keep a poker face in case anyone in the room picked up on his tension.

Sebastian had to think and to think fast. The party was almost over. He had to get Cassie somewhere safe so they could thrash this out. Anger rushed through him at the way she had lied to him, time and time again. She had given herself to him last night while holding this secret. That made him more furious than anything else. She had agreed to an affair with him to ramp up the stakes for him, so that when she dropped her bombshell the person who would pay the biggest price would be him. Damn it, he had already paid the biggest price. She had made sure of it by keeping him in ignorance of his own flesh and blood.

He pushed his anger to one side as he thought about that engaging little boy. *His son.* The words still felt unfamiliar on his tongue, he hadn't expected to say them for many years to come. But there was no mistaking that boy was his. Could no one else see it? *Had* anyone else seen it? His guts turned to gravy just thinking about the fallout from this. He had thought the leak about the Stefani diamond would be devastating, but it didn't even rate next to this.

Sam was a living, breathing image of himself. No wonder he had felt drawn to him. He had felt a connection that was almost visceral.

His stomach twisted again as he saw Cassie and Sam come back to where he was. The child was obviously picking up on the atmosphere; his little chin was trembling and tears began to shine in his eyes. How many times had Sebastian been exactly like that, clinging to his mother, tearful, fearful and unbearably shy?

'Is my mummy in t-trouble?' Sam asked, blinking up at Sebastian. 'She's not going to be taken away again, is she?'

Sebastian felt his heart tighten unbearably. He crouched down and put his hand on the little boy's shoulder, his hand seeming so big in comparison to the small thin bones beneath his palm. 'No one is going to take your mummy away, Sam,' he said, 'but I do need to talk to her. How would you like to come with her to my special hideaway for a few days? Have you ever been on a holiday before?'

Sam shook his head solemnly. 'No...'

Sebastian smiled and gently ruffled the black silk of his hair. 'Then it is about time you did. I will see to it immediately.'

Cassie cleared her throat. 'Excuse me, but I don't want—'

He straightened and cut his eyes to hers, gritting out in an undertone so Sam wouldn't hear, 'Do not speak to me until we are alone. You have a lot of explaining to do and I hope to God you've polished your explanation by the time I hear it or I swear there will be consequences that will not sit well with you.'

Cassie shrank back from the blistering anger in his tone. Her stomach caved in, her knees knocking together as she tried to control her erratic breathing. In spite of his assurances to Sam he could so easily take him off her. It would be the sort of revenge that would appeal to him. He had been denied all knowledge of his son for the first five years of his life. What better way to hurt her than to take Sam away from her indefinitely? She would end up just like Angelica, dragging herself through each day, her heart empty for the son she had lost and most likely would never see again.

Cassie watched in gut-wrenching despair as Sebastian strode over to Stefanos, his aide, exchanging a few words with him before coming back to where she and Sam were standing.

'I have arranged for you and Sam to be transported immediately to Kionia,' he said in a tone that warned her not to interrupt, much less contradict. 'I will contact the orphanage and offer them some excuse as to why you and the boy will not be returning.'

Cassie's eyes flared, but she kept her lips tightly clamped. She could feel the tremble of her son's thin shoulders under her hands and didn't want to cause him any more distress.

'M-Mummy?'

'It's all right, Sam,' she said, stroking his hair with an unsteady hand. 'I'm not going to leave you.'

Sebastian's glittering gaze challenged hers before he squatted down to speak to Sam. 'I have arranged for my old nanny to be at my villa,' he said. 'She will look after you any time Mummy cannot. She is lovely, just like a grandmother.'

'I don't have a grandmother,' Sam said, biting his lip.

Yes, you do, Sebastian thought with a mental wince. His mother was going to take this news hard. She would love Sam, it was not in her nature to do anything else, but accepting Cassie Kyriakis was another thing entirely.

He straightened to his full height to address Cassie once more. 'Stefanos will accompany you to your flat to pick up some essentials, but it is imperative that you speak to no one.'

'But what about Angelica?' she asked. 'I can hardly walk out without some sort of explanation.'

His eyes bored into hers. 'Does she know about this?'

She pressed her lips together, releasing them to whisper, 'No. I've never told her.'

Sebastian felt his spine turn to ice again. 'Does anyone know?' he asked, trying to keep his voice low. 'Anyone at the orphanage?'

She moistened her lips with the point of her tongue.

'Everyone knows he is my son but they don't know who the father is. I swear no one does.'

Sebastian wondered whether he could believe her. She had already told so many lies he was surprised she had been able to keep track of them all. It only demonstrated how adept she was at pulling the wool over everyone's eyes.

'I will see you this evening once you have settled Sam into bed,' he said. 'I have some other engagements now, but Stefanos is doing his utmost to clear my diary for the next few days.'

She gave him a mutinous look but he had already warned Stefanos she might try and escape with the child. He had instructed his aide to put her under lock and key until he returned. He wasn't going to risk anything at this stage. With a few choice words to the press Cassie could have made herself a fortune and brought down his rulership in one fell swoop.

The only question that niggled at him was why hadn't she done so already?

CHAPTER EIGHT

CASSIE paced the floor of the study where Stefanos had instructed her to wait for Sebastian. Sam was in bed, exhausted, barely putting up a struggle when the elderly but totally competent nanny Eleni had told him she would be babysitting him while his mother was downstairs.

Cassie's nerves felt as if they had been stretched beyond the limit. She was jumpy and agitated, the imposing walls of the luxury villa feeling like prison all over again. Her earlier distress had now turned to anger. As each minute dragged past she felt her rage escalating. Was he doing it deliberately? Making her wait for him like this, reminding her with chilling clarity he had all the power, all the control and all the cold-blooded ruthlessness to do what he wanted?

The door suddenly opened and she swung around. 'What the hell do you think you're doing locking me up in this place?' she railed as Sebastian came in.

Cassie had thought she had the highest score on anger until she saw the white-tipped fury on his face. He was in control but barely. She had never seen him so blisteringly, blazingly angry. His whole body was rigid with it, his hands clenched into tight fists, a pulse beating like a jackhammer in his neck.

'You cold-hearted, deceitful little bitch,' he spat at her malevolently.

Cassie took a step backwards, her voice locking in her throat.

He came up close, so close she had to fight every instinct not to shrink away. 'You lying little whore,' he went on brutally. 'I didn't think even you could go as low as you have gone, using a small, innocent child to cover up each and every one of your despicable lies.'

She swallowed tightly as guilt washed over her in scorching waves.

'It was all a game to you, wasn't it?' he said when she didn't speak.

She closed her eyes to escape the fire of his fury.

'Look at me, damn you!'

She flinched and opened her eyes again, her whole body beginning to shake. 'It wasn't like that…'

'What was it like, then?' he said with a curl of his lip. '"Here is a painting by a little orphan,"' he mimicked her voice. 'God, I could shake you until your teeth rattled for that alone.'

Cassie bit the inside of her mouth until she tasted blood.

'You lied to my face time and time again. How could you use a small innocent child to cover your back like that?'

'I know…' she choked. 'I'm sorry…'

His eyes narrowed to black slits. 'You are *sorry*? Oh, so that makes it all OK, then, does it, Cassie? You are sorry you forgot to mention you had my son five years ago but everything's rosy now it's all sorted out.' He raked a hand through his hair. 'God, give me strength.'

'I tried to tell you…I tried to but you didn't respond to my letter.'

His glare turned to a frown. 'Letter?' he asked. 'What letter?'

She swallowed tightly. 'I wrote you a letter as soon as I found out I was pregnant. When you didn't respond I assumed you weren't interested in hearing what I had to tell you. I didn't try again. It was too dangerous in any case. I could hardly write and tell you I was carrying your child—all my letters were screened.'

He gave her a cutting look. 'You were not going to tell me anything until you could do so for maximum effect, isn't that right, Cassie? I am just a matter of weeks away from being crowned as King. You could not have chosen a more devastatingly effective time.'

'No, that's not right,' she said. 'I wasn't going to tell you at all… Sam and I are leaving as soon as my parole is up. I've…I've already got the tickets.'

A menacing silence tightened the air to snapping point.

'So…let me get this right,' he said, skewering her gaze with his. 'You were going to take *my* child off the island never once telling me of his existence, is that correct?'

It sounded awful when he put it like that, Cassie thought. 'I thought it would be for the best,' she said. 'You're about to be King. I thought the last thing you would want to know about is a love-child.'

'Is that what you call him—*a love-child?*' he asked in scorn. 'But there was no love, was there, Cassie?'

She brought up her chin. 'I did love you.' *I do love you.*

His bark of a laugh was a bitter, horrible sound that echoed ominously in the room. 'Oh, yes, I remember now. You claimed to love me but you were opening your legs for anyone else who came along.'

'It wasn't like that…' she said in a barely audible voice. 'There was no one else.'

He came up even closer, so close she could see every dark fleck in his eyes and every spark of glittering hatred. 'Is there no end to your falsehoods?' he bit out. 'Do you think I would fall for any more of your despicable lies?'

Cassie felt the cold hand of despair clutch at her insides. 'I only told you that so I could end our relationship,' she said. 'I was afraid…'

'Of what?'

'Of…of how things were between us,' she said, not able to hold his gaze.

'I don't believe you. I don't believe a word that comes out of that perfidious mouth of yours,' he said. 'You are a liar just as your father always said you were. I was a fool to think otherwise. For years I have thought he was painting a worse picture of you to serve his own ends, but after this I realise everything he said about you was true. You have no conscience, no moral sense of what is right. Lying is second nature to you.'

'Yes, well, he would have known,' she shot back. 'It takes one to know one, doesn't it?'

He gave her a contemptuous look. 'You can malign him all you like because he can't defend himself. I know whose version I prefer to believe.'

Cassie felt her world start to crumble all over again. She had been so close to telling him what her father had been like, had told him more than she had told anyone, and yet now there was no way he would believe her if she told him the rest. The pain she felt was much worse than she could ever have imagined. It was as if her life, all of her suffering and despair had been a fantasy she had made up to protect herself.

Wasn't that always the way it had been? Everyone had always believed her father and they continued to do so even though he was dead. She'd had no one to defend her in the past and there would be no one in the future. Not even the one person she had wanted to understand her situation more than any other.

'Did you know you were pregnant when you ended our relationship?' he asked, still glaring at her furiously.

'No…I only found out after I was in prison. I had a health check done and a pregnancy test was standard procedure. The results came back positive. I was shocked. I didn't even know you could fall pregnant while on the pill.'

Sebastian heard the anguish behind the words and felt his anger loosen around the edges. She had been eighteen years old. Sure, she had acted like a streetwise slut, but finding herself pregnant and in prison must have thrown her for six.

'That's when I wrote to you,' she said, her eyes glistening with moisture. 'I asked to see you. I didn't think it would be appropriate to tell you other than face to face.'

'I received no such letter,' he said, still wondering if he should believe her. She was so good at this, damn her. She could even tear up on cue. He could feel the effect on him and could only assume it was deliberate. What she hoped to achieve he wasn't entirely sure. Perhaps a massive pay out to stop her from going to the press, but if he paid it how could he be sure she wouldn't double-cross him? And besides, he wanted to freely acknowledge Sam as his own son. The child deserved so much better than he'd had so far in his short life.

Sebastian felt his anger simmering all over again at how his son had been born in a prison instead of the palace where he belonged. God only knew what things he had seen or heard in those first formative years of his life, the people he had been housed with, the toughened criminals, the down-and-outs and dregs of society knew his son better than he did.

'You don't believe me, do you?' she said, the line of her mouth bitter.

He hesitated for perhaps a fraction too long to be convincing. 'I can only say if a letter was sent I did not see it. Someone must have intercepted it and destroyed it.'

'Your father?'

Sebastian considered it for a moment. 'I would not like to

think him responsible for such an act, but I have no way of proving it either way.'

'So you'd rather believe me capable of lying than sully your father's name with suspicion.'

He swore under his breath. 'Cassie, you have done nothing but lie to me from the moment we met,' he said. 'If I am having trouble believing you now, then you have only yourself to blame.'

Tears shone in her eyes. 'Please don't take Sam away from me,' she begged. 'He wouldn't cope with it, I know he wouldn't. Please…please don't take him away…'

Sebastian tried to harden his heart but it was impossible. She clearly loved the child and had gone through hell and high water to keep him. 'I am not going to take him away from you,' he said in a gruff tone. 'I can see he loves you as much as you love him. I just want some answers and I want you for once in your life to be honest with me. You surely owe me that?'

'I'm not sure I can trust you,' she said. 'You've brought me here against my will and locked all the doors behind me. I can't bear it.'

'There is no other way,' he said. 'I can't have this leaked out to the press.'

'Is that all that matters to you?' she asked. 'What people will think?'

'Damn it, Cassie, I don't care what people think. I am trying to protect Sam. He is totally innocent in all of this. I have missed out on five years of his life. How can I ever make it up to him? Where the hell do I start?'

Cassie felt so ashamed she hadn't factored in how Sebastian would be feeling right now. He had only just learned of Sam's existence. He had been robbed of so much and it could never be made up to him. She had been robbed herself when Sam had been taken away for the last year of her sentence and look how devastated that had left her. How much worse must he be feeling having not even known he had fathered a child until now?

'I haven't told him you are his father,' she said into the painful silence.

'Were you planning to tell him at some stage?'

'How could I?' she said in a broken whisper.

Sebastian scored another pathway through his hair. His emotions were all over the place. Every bone in his body was aching with the knowledge Cassie had borne his child alone. What if someone *had* intercepted her sole attempt to contact him? How could he blame her for not trying again since her first attempt had yielded nothing? Even her best friend, his sister Lissa, had deserted her at their father's command.

And there was Sam, shy little Sam who looked as if any moment he expected someone to destroy his carefully constructed world. His mother was everything to him, his anchor, just as Sebastian's mother had been to him. How could he swoop in and take control without considering the effect on that endearing little boy?

'He needs to be told,' he said heavily. 'I would like to be the one to do so.'

Cassie looked at him with worry, a dark shadow in her green eyes. 'You mean to acknowledge him as your own?'

He placed his closed fist against his heart. 'He is *my son*, Cassie,' he said. 'Do you really think I would turn my back on him?'

'No…it's just I thought with the coronation and all…'

'That is not important right now,' he said. 'I want to spend the next couple of weeks getting to know him. I have to come to some sort of decision over his future as well as my own.'

'I'm not asking you to give up the throne,' she said. 'I would never ask that of you.'

He studied her for a lengthy pause. 'Why did you agree to

another affair with me?' he asked. 'You knew I was his father—why dance with danger by getting involved with me again?'

She bit her lip and lowered her gaze. 'I knew it was dangerous but…'

'But?'

She brought her eyes back to his. 'I couldn't help myself…'

Sebastian hoped it wasn't another one of her lies. She looked exhausted, pale and fragile and nothing like the in-your-face Cassie of the past. She had been steadily shrinking from him from the moment he had stepped into the room, cowering almost, which made him wonder…

'Do you mind if I go to bed?' she asked, pinching at the bridge of her nose. 'I have the most appalling headache. It's been coming on all afternoon.'

'I didn't realise,' he said, frowning in concern. 'You should have said. I will get Stefanos to show you to your room. It is next door to Sam's and close to mine if you need anything during the night.'

'Thank you…'

'Cassie?'

She turned and looked at him, her face bleak and her eyes nothing less than soulless. 'Yes?'

'Thank you for not getting rid of him,' he said. 'You would have had many reasons to do so, but you did not.'

'I *could* not,' she said almost fiercely. 'Termination or adoption was never going to be an option for me. I had grown up without knowing my mother. It's been like a gaping hole in my life. I couldn't bear for my child to suffer the same.'

Sebastian could sense the pain behind the quietly spoken words. How had he not seen this about her before? But then he reminded himself their clandestine meetings had always been about satisfying an urgent physical need, they had not been about discovering intimate details of each other's lives.

He suddenly realised he had told her even less about his own life. He hadn't shared his frustration over his father's heavy handedness. He had told her nothing of the sense of duty that was at times burdensome. He had simply enjoyed a red-hot affair with her, not for a moment thinking she was anything but a good-time girl.

Sebastian could see how fragile she was now. She looked like a wraith with her too-slim body and long, blonde hair awry from dragging her fingers through it agitatedly. It awoke every protective instinct in his body to draw her close and offer what comfort he could.

'Cassie.' He reached out and touched her ever so gently on the arm, but she flinched away as if he had slapped her.

She looked at him, her tear-washed eyes glittering with a last stand show of defiance. 'I don't want to talk any more. I'm tired and my head feels as if it's going to explode. If you had a decent bone in your body you'd realise that and let me go to bed.'

He held her challenging glare for a moment before he let out a weary sigh. 'Of course,' he said, holding the door open for her. '*Kalinichta,* Cassie.'

She didn't respond, which he more or less expected, but it disappointed him all the same. He saw the shadows in her emerald eyes and knew he had played a huge part in putting them there. Now he wanted to know how on earth he was going to remove them.

CHAPTER NINE

CASSIE wasn't sure what had woken her only an hour or so later. The silence most probably, she thought wryly as she threw back the covers to go and check on Sam, who was sleeping next door. After years in a noisy prison she still found the quietness of night faintly disturbing.

She gently pushed open the door of Sam's room but came to a startled halt when she saw who was sitting beside the bed, with one of Sam's tiny hands cupped in his. 'Is…is everything all right?' she said in a low whisper.

Sebastian tucked Sam's hand back under the covers. 'Yes…I was just…checking him before I went to bed.'

Cassie waited until they were out in the corridor before she spoke. 'Haven't you been to bed yet? It's way past midnight.'

He rubbed one of his hands down his face, the scrape of his palm over his stubble sounding loud in the silence. 'No, I had some things to see to,' he said. 'How is your headache?'

Somehow the genuine concern in his voice made Cassie's skin tingle with awareness. So too did the fact she was standing before him in an almost sheer slip of a night-gown with only a light bathrobe covering it. 'It's gone… sort of…'

He lifted a hand and gently brushed back the hair off her

face, his touch so light she felt every nerve spring to life. She stood stock-still, not breathing, not thinking—just feeling.

'Do you fancy a drink or something?' he asked in a brusque tone, shoving his hand in his pocket as if he regretted touching her. 'I was just about to go downstairs and make one.'

She lifted her brows. 'You fix your own drinks?'

'Occasionally,' he said, his expression locking her out. 'Just because I have a late night doesn't mean my staff have to as well.'

'Did Sam call out?' she asked as he led the way downstairs. 'I checked him before I went to bed and he was fine.'

'No, he didn't call out,' he said. 'I just wanted to sit with him.'

'Oh…'

His eyes met hers. 'I do have the right to sit with him, do I not?'

'Of course…I didn't mean to suggest—'

He held open the door of one of the reception rooms, his eyes still boring into hers. 'There is no question over my paternity, is there, Cassie?'

Cassie felt the question like a slap across the face. 'No…there's no question at all.'

He studied her for a stretched-out moment. 'Under the circumstances royal protocol might call for proof.'

She held his piercing dark gaze, her heart contracting at the lack of trust she could see in his eyes. 'Go right ahead,' she said, stalking over to the middle of the room. 'I have nothing to hide.'

'Ah, but that is not quite true, is it, Cassie?' he said, coming over to where she was standing. 'You are rather adept at hiding things from me.'

Cassie took an unsteady step backwards. 'I told you I tried to tell you about Sam…'

'I am not just talking about Sam.'

She swept her tongue across her lips, her eyes automatically darting to the door. 'W-what are you talking about, then?'

'There,' he said. 'You did it just then. You get this cornered look in your eyes as if you think I am going to take a swipe at you. I used to think it was because of what went on in prison, but while I was thinking through some things this evening I realised I had seen that look on your face before.'

She straightened her shoulders with an effort. 'You have a rather threatening demeanour at times, Sebastian.'

'I would *never* raise my hand in anger,' he said, frowning darkly. 'You surely know that, Cassie. Have I ever given you a reason to think otherwise?'

'No…no, of course not,' Cassie said, thinking of how gentle he had been with Sam so far.

He seemed satisfied with her answer and after a moment he moved across to a drinks servery and poured some juice for her and a cognac for himself. 'Have you had time to have a look around while you have been here today?' he asked as he handed her the glass. 'It occurred to me that I didn't show you around last time you were here.'

'Not really,' she said, taking the drink from him. 'I wanted to spend the time settling Sam in—he was a bit nervous about coming here. Besides, I didn't want to get us both lost looking around by ourselves, and I wasn't sure what to say to the staff or what they knew about us so we kept to our rooms.'

'Eleni and, of course, Stefanos know Sam is my son, and the housekeeper who has worked here for most of my life, but that is all,' Sebastian said. 'I will take Sam on a tour tomorrow so he feels more secure. Finish your drink and I will show you around this floor. I think you will enjoy the views.'

Cassie followed him into the next room where the views from the large windows overlooking the ocean were stunningly beautiful, especially in the silvery darkness of a moonlit night. Lights from one of the passenger ferries to Greece or Turkey could be seen twinkling in the distance.

'Let me show you the view from one of the east-facing rooms,' Sebastian said. 'You can see the Port of Aquila on Calista.'

Cassie followed him into another room, which she took to be the morning room as there was an informal dining setting, as well as a large, comfortable-looking sofa where she could imagine members of the royal family would peruse the newspapers. He was right about the view, she thought as she looked at the angry sea below.

'As you see, it is very private,' Sebastian said from her left shoulder. 'The cliffs and rocks below make it impossible for anyone to access the grounds from the three seaboard sides.'

Cassie could feel the warmth of him standing so close and the deep timbre of his voice was like the melodious rumble of organ pipes. 'It is very beautiful here,' she said, more to fill the silence than anything else. 'And, as you say, very private.'

'Privacy is more valuable than you can ever imagine for people like me,' he said, still looking at the view. 'In fact I cannot put a price on it.'

Cassie picked up the wistfulness in his tone and turned to look at him, a small frown tugging at her brow. 'You sound as if you are not looking forward to being crowned as King and all it entails.'

He shifted his gaze from the window to mesh with hers, the edginess she had always associated with him evident in the way he held himself. 'No, that is not true,' he said. 'I am well prepared for the role and have looked forward to it for most of my life, but there are times...' He lifted one of his broad shoulders in a shrug that communicated everything and nothing.

'But there are times?' Cassie prodded.

His eyes moved away from hers. 'Come,' he said. 'I think you would like the library and the music room. Do you still play the piano?'

'I haven't touched one in years,' Cassie said as he led her to another room towards the western end of the house. 'I wasn't all that great at it in any case. I only did it because my father for…I mean…thought it was an essential part of a young lady's upbringing to have some proficiency in the arts.'

Sebastian held the music-room door open for her, noting how she had stumbled over her choice of words. He breathed in her scent as she walked past, a mixture of her heady jasmine and his sharp citrus that unleashed a host of memories from the lockers of his mind. He had showered every time they had made love in the past, but he could have sworn there were still times he could smell her in the very pores of his skin. He could still smell her on him from last night. 'Play something for me,' he said, letting the door close on a soft click behind him. 'Something to suit your current mood.'

Her eyes flicked to his, a camera-shutterlike look passing through them before they fell away and rested on the white grand piano. 'I'm not sure I can remember anything by ear…' she said, her teeth worrying at her bottom lip, her arms wrapped around her body like a shield.

Sebastian watched as she circled the instrument, like a wary opponent facing a much-feared foe. 'It's not going to bite you if you touch it, Cassie,' he said softly.

He strode over and pulled out the stool for her and once she was seated, or rather perched on the edge of it, he lifted the lid so the sound could reverberate throughout the spacious room.

Cassie opened and closed her fingers, her pulse like a drum beneath her skin. For someone who had lived the life of a party girl she knew she was doing a very poor job of playing the role now. She hated playing in front of an audience. She had only once played in front of Sebastian in the past and that had been entirely by accident. The apartment he had borrowed from a friend for their secret trysts had an old, slightly out of tune upright piano, and, arriving earlier than him one day, Cassie had sat down and run her normally rigid-with-fear fingers over the keys. Even she had been surprised by the poignancy of the cadences she had played, and it had been some minutes before she had realised Sebastian had been leaning against the door jamb, his dark, penetrating gaze focussed on her as he listened…

Cassie pulled away from the past and placed her fingers on the keys and started to play, stumblingly at first, hesitantly, like a small child at her first pianoforte exam. She had to remind herself her father was dead. He couldn't break a ruler over her knuckles now if she tripped over a note. He couldn't shout from another room with biting criticisms of her technique. He couldn't storm into the room and slam the lid down on the piano so hard she almost lost control of her insides in the most humiliating way of all.

No, he was rotting in hell where he belonged. Tears suddenly blurred her vision, but she played on, the notes rising and falling with each aching breath she took, her heart taking up far too much room in her chest as she thought of all she'd had in her hands and thrown away like stale bread crusts to the seagulls nesting on the cliffs below the windows.

Sebastian found himself transfixed. It was not just the music that was unusually poignant, but it was the fleeting shadows on Cassie's beautiful, model-perfect face. He was close enough to see the tears rolling down her cheeks, as if the music had touched her in a way she had not intended or indeed expected it to.

She had never cried in front of him in the past, not openly at least. He was well used to female tears having grown up with sisters; he understood more than most about the shifting of hormones and the moods that came and went like the tides. But that was a side he had never seen in Cassie. She had always been so in control emotionally, or had she? The devil-may-care attitude she had brandished about in the past was no longer a part of who she was now. She was quieter, watchful and deeper, like a shallow, bubbling brook that had suddenly turned a corner and become a deeply flowing river instead.

Careful, he lectured himself as another trill of notes sent the hairs on his arms upright. She was not for ever; she was just for now. He had to remember that, even if some secret part of him would have liked things to be different. He wouldn't have been the first royal to marry a commoner, but Cassie's past made any such alliance impossible. Was that why he was feeling this burning ache in his throat?

She looked so beautiful sitting there like that, her long slim fingers dancing over the keys as her confidence increased. He recognised a few bars of a Beethoven sonata but she suddenly stumbled over a note and froze like one of the marble statues in the gallery three rooms away.

'Cassie?' He stepped towards her.

She got to her feet, the piano stool almost toppling backwards in her haste. 'I'm sorry…' she said, not quite meeting his eyes. 'I was never very good at that piece. Too many sharps and flats…or something…'

Sebastian was beginning to think 'or something' just about summed Cassie Kyriakis up. He drew out a clean handkerchief, and came over to where she was standing with her arms folded across her chest, and gently dabbed at the tears on her cheeks. 'I think you played rather beautifully, Cassie,' he said. 'I didn't realise you were so talented. That is yet another secret you have kept from me.'

Her eyes watered up again, but before he could attend to the damage she took his handkerchief from him with a slight brush of her fingers against his, a rueful twist contorting the fullness of her mouth. 'Do you mind if I find somewhere to freshen up?' she asked.

Sebastian felt that tight knot in his throat again. She was holding him off; he wasn't sure why. Had he slipped under her guard, seeing more than she wanted him to see? So many clues were starting to make sense, like a crossword that had long been unsolved due to an unknown word. He could force it out of her, or he could wait for her to tell him. Something told him force was not the way to go. If what she had hinted at was true, and he was starting to suspect it was, she would need time and gentle handling to feel safe enough to reveal the full extent of her past.

'Sure,' he said, and led the way back out of the music room to the sweeping staircase. 'There is a guest bathroom on the next floor, second on the right. Take your time.'

She stretched her lips into a smile that looked almost painful. 'Thank you.'

He felt a heavy sigh bring his shoulders down once she had gracefully ascended the stairs, the invisible atoms of her perfume teasing his nostrils long after she had disappeared from sight…

Cassie leant back on the bathroom door and slowly slid to the floor, her head going forward on her bent knees, her shoulders shaking as she wrestled her emotions back into the steel chains she had long ago locked them in.

Who was she fooling? How could she possibly expect to be in Sebastian's presence after last night and not feel vulnerable? It wasn't just about him now knowing about Sam. She had been far too vulnerable when it came to Sebastian Karedes right from the start. But it was far worse now than it had ever been. He was starting to see things she had desperately kept hidden before. She had felt it in his steady, watchful gaze downstairs; the quizzical flicker in his eyes every now and again, as if he was trying to put a rather complicated puzzle together.

Cassie almost laughed out loud as she dragged herself to her feet. A puzzle, that was what she was. No one could figure her out because she liked it that way. What alternative did she have anyway? Who was going to believe her now?

There was a knock at the door and she almost leapt out of her skin. 'Cassie?' Sebastian's voice sounded out with deep strains of concern in it. 'Are you all right in there?'

She quickly blew her nose and tossed the tissue in the bin. 'I'm fine,' she said and came out, closing the door softly behind her.

The silence was like a mantle settling about them. Cassie could feel the soft cloak of muted light surrounding them. Shadows danced off the walls, tempting, taunting shadows that made her aware of how isolated they were. Sam was asleep upstairs with Eleni close by. There was no one around, no bodyguards, no lurking members of the press, just the silence and her lingering memory of last night in his arms. Could he feel it? she wondered. Was that why he was looking at her that way? His dark eyes scanning her features, as if looking for a chink in her hastily assembled armour?

'I have something to show you,' he said. 'It's in my room along the hall.'

Cassie put her hands up. 'Oh, no, you don't,' she said, backing away. 'Don't try that line with me. It's so hackneyed. I'm going to see your etchings or your anything just so you can fast track me back into your bed.'

He lifted one brow at her. 'You think that's what I was doing?'

She gave him a narrow-eyed look. 'I *know* that's what you were doing. Go on, admit it. You were going to lure me into your parlour and one kiss would lead to another and then we both know what would happen. I told you last night was a mistake. We should never have given into the temptation.'

'Last night was not a mistake,' he said. 'I wanted you and you wanted me. Nothing has changed, Cassie.'

Cassie plugged her ears with her fingers. 'Stop it. Stop it right now, do you hear me?'

He pulled her hands down from her face. 'No,' he said, suddenly deadly serious again. 'You stop it and listen to me. *I want you.*' He spaced out the words for maximum effect and Cassie had to fight not to weaken as he continued. 'I know it's crazy and probably downright dangerous but I want you so badly it's like a pain in my gut that won't go away.'

Emotion clogged her throat. 'Please, Sebastian…' Her voice dropped to a desperate whisper. 'You don't know what you're doing…it's hormones…or something.'

He gave her a little shake and saw the flare of her eyes, felt the stiffening of her body and the quiver of her bottom lip before she got it under control. 'It's the "or something" I am worried about,' he said heavily, resting his forehead against hers. 'What am I going to do with you, Caz, my beautiful, complicated chameleon? What on earth am I going to do with you, hmm?'

Cassie felt like candle wax melting under a powerful heat source. Her bones loosened, her ligaments softened, her heart swelled and her resolve…well, it had been a little off centre in any case. 'You have to let me go,' she said, but it didn't sound anywhere near as convincing as she had wanted it to, it was too whispery, too don't-take-me-seriously-when-I-say-this. 'Now…right now…before we go in any deeper.'

It seemed a long time before he lifted his forehead from hers. He drew in a breath, an uneven one, which surprised her for she had thought it was just she who was struggling to keep the past back where it belonged.

He stepped back, just one step but it seemed as if a chasm had opened up between them. 'I was going to show you a photograph,' he said. 'In my bedroom, I have a photograph of you

I took one day when you weren't watching. I have never shown it to you. I didn't get the chance.'

Cassie's eyes went wide and her heart began to stutter, not unlike her voice. 'You...y-you have a photograph of me? You mean you didn't have a ritual burning when I dumped you?'

He winced at her choice of words. 'You know something? I hate that word. Dumped.' He spat it out like a mouthful of something vile.

She gave him an irritated look. 'Ended our relationship, then. Called it quits. Broke it off. Told you it was over.'

'But it's not over, is it, Cassie?' he asked in a low deep tone that sent a shower of remembered sensations down the entire length of her spine.

Cassie gritted her teeth. 'I *want* it to be over. Do you think I want to feel like this? You look at me like that and I—' She stopped, suddenly realising how she was betraying herself to him.

He stepped closer, just that one step but it bridged the chasm again. His body heat was searing a way through her clothes; his eyes were burning with promise, the promise of passion and paradise.

'And you what, Cassie?' he asked in that same sun-warmed satin-sliding-over-bare-skin tone.

Cassie sucked in a ragged breath and threw caution to the winds still raging outside. 'And I want you...' she said, not a whisper, not loud, but somewhere right in between.

The air was heavy, the silence so thick she could almost reach out and touch it. Instead she reached out and touched him, on the face, the soft skin of her palm making a raspy sound on the stubble that had grown there since he had shaved that morning.

She wasn't sure who made the next move after that. She had a sneaking suspicion it might have been her, but her conscience later on wouldn't allow her to admit it. Suddenly their mouths were fused, their bodies locked tightly together, their hands moving in wild, frantic desperation to get as close as humanly possible.

Cassie opened her mouth to the driving thrust of his tongue, met it with hers, tangling, teasing, tasting the promise of what was to come. She felt the surge of sexual energy streak through her body like a fire racing through thick, dry scrub, flames of need licking at every pleasure point in anticipation of his touch.

He had backed her against the nearest wall, his pelvis rock hard against her, grinding, pushing and probing until she wanted to scream with frustration at not having him where she wanted him most.

He lifted his mouth off hers long enough to say, 'I told myself it wasn't going to be like this.'

'Like what?' she asked, running her tongue over her lips and savouring the sex and salt male taste of him.

His eyes were so dark and intense as they held hers. 'In the past it was always so rushed between us,' he said, nipping at her bottom lip, tug, pull, tug, pull. 'Last night was the same. I told myself the next time together would be slow and sensual and something that neither of us will ever forget.'

Cassie didn't want to be reminded this was not going to be for ever. It was a just-in-the-moment thing. She knew that, but it was hard to think clearly when his teeth were doing that thing with her bottom lip and his hands searching for her breasts through the light but still annoying barrier of her clothes.

She reached down to stroke him through his trousers, the hard outline of his erection pulsing against her touch, reminding her of how big he was, and how her body, as slim as it was, had always managed to accommodate him.

Sebastian dragged his mouth off hers again. 'Not here,' he

said. 'Not here in the hall. I want you in my bed this time. Not against the wall, not against the kitchen bench, not in some cramped corner of someone else's house, but in my bed.'

Cassie brought his mouth back down to hers. 'A bed would be nice,' she murmured throatily.

'That's usually where this happens first,' he said, nuzzling against her neck. 'I don't think we've been together in a bed before.'

'Then it's about time we did something about that,' she said, sliding her hands down his chest as she popped each button on his shirt.

He shrugged himself out of it, and, kicking it aside with his foot, scooped her up in his arms and carried her to a room several doors down. He shouldered the door open in a classical-hero sort of way that did serious damage to Cassie's heart rate.

The mattress was soft, but he was rock-hard when he came down on top of her. 'You've got too many clothes on,' she said, tugging at his belt.

'So have you,' he said, and removed the problem with a deftness that was exhilarating.

Skin on skin.

Cassie could feel the pores of her skin opening to take more of him in. She could smell the musk of his body, the heat of it was driving her wild, but he was slowing down. She could sense it; each kiss was no less drugging but it was softer, lingering. Each caress of his hands was drawing out her response in a torturous way she had never experienced with him before. He cupped her breasts, rubbing his thumbs over the aching, tight points so leisurely she began to whimper in impatience. She wanted to feel his hot, moist mouth sucking hard on her nipples, to feel the almost savage scrape of his teeth, to feel the answering tug of her feminine muscles crying out to be stretched to the limit. She opened her thighs but he didn't do what she wanted or expected. He kept kissing her, on her mouth, her neck, her ear lobes, her collarbones and her breasts until she was panting and squirming and as close to begging as her pride would allow.

'I know what you want but I am not giving it to you,' he said, looking at her smoulderingly in between kisses. 'Or at least not yet.'

She arched her spine in an effort to search for his probing heat but, for the first time in her experience with him, failing. 'If you don't get inside me this minute I am going to…to…'

His laugh was a low rumble that made her longing for him all the more intense. 'To what, Cassie? Tonight I am going to take as long as I damn well like.'

Cassie smothered a groan of restlessness and gave herself up to the go-slow rhythm he was setting.

There was something to be said about taking your time, she decided a few breathless minutes later. She was becoming aware of her body in a way she had not done so before, even with him. She felt the flow of her blood to her feminine core, the way it swelled and ached and pulsed to be caressed. She shifted beneath him, trying to get him to give into the temptation of driving into her but he wouldn't do it. He kept moving away, not far, but just enough to make sure she felt the throb of his body, but not his full possession.

'You are doing this on purpose,' she said, mock-glaring at him even as she clutched at him. 'You want me to beg, don't you?'

He smiled and bent his head back to her breast, suckling, teasing and finally biting until every nerve in her body jumped to attention. 'If it's any comfort to you I'm having a hard time keeping control,' he said. 'I want to take you to the heights like I did last night, but I am not going to do it. Not this time.'

This last time… The words almost echoed in the silence.

Cassie shoved the reality aside. 'Do it now or don't do it at all,' she said with a steely glint in her eyes.

'You don't mean that,' he said, trailing a blistering pathway of kisses down past her belly button to the humid heart of her.

'Sure I d-do,' she said, sucking in a breath when his lips skated over her swollen folds. 'It's a woman's prerogative to change her mind at any time during the procedure.'

'I know the law, Caz,' he said, softly parting her. 'God, you are like an orchid, so beautiful.'

Cassie had always struggled with body issues. She'd had no idea how delicately she was made; the tidy secrets of her body were so different from his. There was no way he could hide his reaction to her, but she could hide hers from him, but only just.

Somehow she thought that was a good thing in the design of things. Women were far more vulnerable when it came to sex. She *felt* something when she shared her body with Sebastian. It was visceral, instinctive and totally consuming. Her heart was in it just as much as her body. She wouldn't be doing this now if she didn't care about him. It was a going-nowhere love, but this night would have to last for ever.

She knew that—he knew that.

She would *make* it last for ever.

She had gone through six years of hell and managed to survive. Another sixty or so wouldn't be easy, but at least she had loved and lost—it was supposed to be better than not loving at all, but somehow she seriously doubted it.

Cassie was jerked back to the moment when his tongue entered her, a lick first, then a gentle probe, and then a sensual onslaught that had her spine arching off the bed as an orgasm ripped through her unlike anything she had felt before. She gasped her way through it, her body disconnected from her mind as the sensations rocketed through her, leaving her boneless and shuddering with aftershocks.

'Good?' he asked with a smile that should have looked supercilious, but somehow didn't.

'Better than good,' she gasped out. 'One of the best…'

He moved up her body until he was within striking distance of hers. 'I think we should put that to the test, don't you?' he asked.

Cassie was almost beyond words. Her body was limp, but somehow still needy in spite of the earth-shattering response he had summoned from her. She watched as he applied a condom, the engorged length of him exciting her all over again.

He moved over her, his weight balanced on his elbows, his eyes glittering with need as he gently nudged her thighs apart. She arched her spine to receive that first wonderful thrust of his powerfully made body, a gasp escaping from her mouth as he began a torturously slow rhythm. Cassie dug her fingers into his buttocks, every sensitised nerve in her body begging for more speed to increase the delicious friction. He gradually increased his pace, his breathing becoming more hectic, and she knew with certainty he was coming closer and closer to losing control. She could feel the tension building in him, the muscles beneath her fingers tightly clenched before he took that final plunge. She was with him all the way, her hips rising to meet the downward thrust of his. She hit the summit first but he was right behind her, the shudders of his body as he emptied himself making her shiver all over.

Cassie listened to the sound of their breathing, wondering if he would say something, *anything* to fill the lengthening silence. But after a while she gave up thinking about it. She lay with him still enclosed within her, his face pressed against her neck, his warm breath tickling her skin as her eyelids gradually drifted down in total blissful relaxation…

Sebastian gently eased himself off her, disposing of the condom before he came back to stroke the tussled hair back off her face. Her soft mouth was swollen from his kisses, the faint flush of sexual pleasure still evident in her cheeks. This was the Cassie he had grown to love in the past. Only when her guard was down like this did he get a tiny glimpse of who she really was. She was complex, not shallow, she was troubled, not a trouble-maker, she was his Caz, the woman he could never have.

She stirred beneath him, her eyes opening to meet his. 'Seb?'

His smile was crooked. 'It's been a long time since you called me that.'

She touched his face with her fingertips, a feather-light caress that made his skin lift. 'That's because we can't go back,' she said with a hint of sadness in her voice. 'We're not Caz and Seb now. We're Cassie the ex-criminal and Sebastian the Prince Regent of Aristo, and never the twain shall meet, as they say.'

'It's not enough, Cassie,' he said, running his tongue across his lips as he looked deep into her eyes. 'I want more.'

Cassie swallowed tightly, hope like a raising agent in her chest. 'What do you mean?'

His expression was rueful as he tucked a strand of her hair back behind her ear. 'I thought once we did this a couple of times it would be enough, but it's not. I want you again.'

She stared at him, suspended between hope and despair. 'I'm not sure what to say…' she took another small swallow and added '…or what you are saying…'

He pressed a soft kiss to her mouth, a brush-like touch that made her lips tingle. 'I would like to have more time, Caz,' he said, 'a few more nights alone with you. That is all I am asking.'

'Why?' Cassie asked.

He raked a hand through his hair and let out a deep, uneven sigh. 'Because for the first time since I met you six years ago I am starting to see a glimpse of who you really are. I want to see more.'

Cassie lowered her gaze from his, her heart aching and heavy in her chest. 'There's no future in this, you know that. There can never be anything but an affair between us.' *And a very short and secret one at that,* she thought with another pang of despair.

He kissed her softly, lingeringly, before pushing up her chin to meet her eyes once more. 'Let's have what we can have for as long as we can have it,' he said.

Cassie left it far too late to say no. For a few pulsing seconds she had her chance, but she said nothing. But as his mouth came back down to claim hers she knew exactly why she hadn't.

She still loved him.

CHAPTER TEN

CASSIE was helping Sam with his breakfast the next morning when Sebastian came in. She looked up, knowing her cheeks were glowing from all the intimacy they had shared during the night before she had slipped back to her own room in the early hours of the morning while he had been sleeping.

He met her gaze for a pulsing moment before turning to Sam. 'Good morning, Sam,' he said, taking the chair beside him. 'Did you sleep well?'

Sam put his spoon down politely. 'Yes. I could hear the sea. Mummy said I might be able to go to the beach and build a sandcastle.'

'I think that would be a very good idea,' Sebastian said. 'But first I would like to talk to you about something very important.'

Sam's big brown eyes instantly clouded with worry. He looked at his mother, his chin starting to tremble. 'Have I d-done something wrong?' he asked in a thin voice.

Sebastian felt his chest tighten and took both of Sam's small hands in his, again marvelling at how tiny they were compared to his own. He looked into those deeply brown eyes so like his own and wondered if that haunted, terrified look was the outcome of his early years living in prison. How could he make his little boy feel secure? It would take months if not years and yet he had so little time at his disposal. 'You have done nothing wrong, Sam,' he said gently. Oh, God, where did he begin? How could he tell this small innocent child how he had let him and his mother down?

Five years,

He had missed it all. He hadn't even seen a photograph of Sam as a baby. He hadn't even thought to ask Cassie to show him one. Not that he had given her much of a chance to retrieve any. He had packed her and Sam away with barely enough time for Cassie to pack a few belongings together and tell her flatmate where she and Sam were going.

'Sam…' He cleared his throat and began again, 'I have recently found out I am your father.'

Sam glanced at his mother. 'But I don't have a father, do I, Mummy?'

Sebastian saw Cassie's throat move up and down. 'Darling…I have never actually said you didn't have a father…'

'No, but Spiro said I didn't have one,' Sam said. 'I heard him tell Kara.'

Cassie frowned. 'What did he say?'

Sam bit his lip. 'He said it was anyone's guess who I belonged to…'

Sebastian met Cassie's bleak gaze before turning back to Sam. 'You belong to me, Sam,' he said, giving the boy's hands a gentle squeeze. 'You will always belong to me, no matter what happens in the future.'

Cassie felt her stomach clench with dread. What was he implying? That any future of Sam's would be with his father and not with her? What else could he mean? There was no way Sebastian could have it all. They both knew that. That was why last night had been so poignant to her. This next couple of weeks would be all they would ever have together, as a little family. It would all too soon be over.

'So you and Mummy and me are going to always be together?' Sam asked with hope shining in his eyes.

'For the time being at least,' Sebastian said after a slight pause.

Sam's eyes began to water. 'Is Mummy going to leave me here?'

'No,' Cassie said stridently, glaring at Sebastian.

Sebastian put his hands on Sam's shoulders. 'Sam, I know this is hard for you to understand, but your mother and I are not married. But that does not mean we both don't love you. We do, very much.'

Sam gulped back a little sob. 'But I don't want to be anywhere without my mummy,' he said. 'Can't we stay with you? We won't get in the way, will we, Mummy?'

Cassie bit the inside of her mouth to stop herself from crying. 'Sweetie, it's not that simple…'

Sam's eyes were streaming now and his bottom lip trembling as he slipped off the chair and came over to her. 'But why can't you marry Daddy and then we can all live together?' he asked. 'I like it here. I can see boats from my bedroom window and there's a big garden. Eleni said there's even a pool.'

Cassie kept her eyes away from Sebastian's as she bent down and hugged Sam. 'Darling, your father is a very important man. It's just not possible for him to live with us all the time. He has to travel all over the world sometimes. But I am sure we'll sort something out, something that makes all of us happy.'

'I don't want to go back to the orphanage,' Sam said, starting to cry. 'I want to stay here with Daddy and you.'

Sebastian rubbed at his face, his throat tightening as he thought of how different things could have been if he had known six years ago what he knew now. He would have done anything to have avoided the pain he could see etched on his little boy's face. What sort of father did Sam think he was that he hadn't done a single thing so far to give him what he was entitled to?

Cassie was looking daggers at him, piercing him with silent blame for upsetting their child, and Sebastian could hardly blame her. He had handled things appallingly. Sam was far too young to understand the dynamics of the situation. He would need careful nurturing and protection until something could be sorted out.

For so long the search for the Stefani diamond and Sebastian's future coronation as King had been his entire focus. He had thought of nothing else but how he could lead his people, and yet now he was faced with an agonising decision.

How could he take Sam away from his mother, even for an access visit? Sam was insecure and painfully shy. Besides, what little boy didn't need their mother at that age?

And then there was Cassie. The young woman Sebastian had never been able to erase from his mind. The last two nights had brought it all back, the way she made him feel, the passion that flared so hotly between them. He had been surprised at how disappointed he had felt when he had woken to find she had gone back to her room some time during the early hours of the morning. He had lain there in amongst the crumpled bedclothes, breathing in her scent, his body aching to possess her all over again.

The people of Aristo would never accept her as his bride. They were going to have enough trouble accepting her as the mother of his son. Cassie's past was always going to be a stumbling block. But last night at the piano he had seen a side to her that was as far from the party-girl socialite as anyone could be. It made him wonder if he had been too hasty in his judgement of her, in fact if everyone had been too hasty. There was a haunting sadness about her, he had been noticing it more and more, especially when she thought he wasn't watching.

Eleni came in at that moment and with a few cheery words with Sam led him away to play with some toys she had found in the nursery upstairs.

Cassie turned and glared at him. 'Couldn't you have waited until Sam was feeling a little more settled before dumping all that on him?' she asked.

Sebastian raked his hand through his hair. 'What was I supposed to do?' he asked. 'There is no point lying to him. I am his father and I want him to know and accept that.'

'You wanted to stake your claim on him, that's what you wanted,' she said, flashing her emerald gaze at him. 'I won't let you take him away from me, Sebastian.'

'I am not going to do anything that will not be of benefit to my son,' he said.

Her eyes flared. 'Oh, and what is that supposed to mean? That it will be of much greater benefit to him to be away from his jailbird mother?'

'I didn't say that, Cassie.'

'You didn't have to,' she said. 'I can see it every time you look at me. You are thinking how the hell am I going to tell the world who the mother of my son is—isn't that right, Sebastian?'

He set his jaw. 'Look, Cassie, this is a difficult situation for both of us. I have so little time in which to get to know Sam before I have to announce his existence. I have missed out on so much and I need to do what I can to make up for it. Do you realise I haven't even seen a photograph of him as a baby?'

Her stiff stance relaxed a little. 'I brought some photographs with me,' she said. 'I grabbed them when Stefanos took us via the flat.'

Sebastian was surprised she had thought to do so, especially given the haste in which he had insisted his orders be carried out. 'I would like to see them,' he said, trying to disguise the lump that had risen in his throat.

'I'll get them,' she said. 'They're in my room.'

Sebastian's mobile started to ring and he unhooked it from his belt and glanced at the screen. 'I'll have to get this, I'm afraid,' he said. 'Can you find your way to my study? I'll meet you there in ten minutes.'

She gave a nod and slipped out of the room while Sebastian took the call, keeping his voice low as he spoke to Stefanos. There was still no news about the Stefani diamond but neither had there been anything leaked to the press about Sam. There were some photographs in the paper of the party and a short piece about Sebastian's role as royal patron, but thankfully nothing else, so far.

Cassie took the scrapbooks she had made and after a few wrong turns made her way to Sebastian's study. She stood outside for a moment, holding the books against her chest, trying to prepare herself for yet another emotional journey through time. Every time she looked at the photos documenting Sam's life she felt such an aching sadness that she hadn't been able to give him a normal start to life. Everything had been against her from the very start. Sam had opened his eyes inside the walls of a bleak prison, not in the richly furnished palace where by blood he belonged. There had been no one with her when she had given birth after twenty agonising hours of labour, no one but a gruff midwife and a particularly unsympathetic prison guard who had stood and watched every intimate detail with a sneering expression on her face.

Cassie had longed for Sebastian to suddenly burst through the door and come to her. She'd had to bite down on her lip until it was bleeding to stop from crying out for him as every contraction had rippled through her abdomen.

She had never missed her mother more than at that point when Sam had finally been handed to her. She had never even held a baby before, never knew how tiny they were, how vulnerable and precious and totally innocent. Had her mother lived long enough to hold her? she wondered. No one had ever told her. Had her mother looked down at her as she had looked down at Sam at that moment, and sworn to love and protect her baby no matter what?

The door of the study suddenly opened in front of her. 'How long have you been standing there?' Sebastian asked with narrowed eyes.

Cassie clutched the scrapbooks against her chest, her mouth going dry at the hardened look in his eyes. 'Not long… I got lost a couple of times on the way down…'

He held her gaze for an infinitesimal moment, before indicating for her to go inside. He raked a hand through his hair in that edgy way of his. 'I have a lot on my mind right now.'

'I can come back later if you would prefer,' she said, glancing back at the door.

'No.' He dropped his hand from where it had been to rub the back of his neck, the smile he gave her a little forced. 'Take a seat on the sofa. Would you like coffee or tea? I suddenly realised I interrupted your breakfast.'

'No, I'm fine…thank you…' Cassie sat on the sofa and held her breath as he took the seat beside her, his thigh brushing against hers.

'Show me,' he said, his voice sounding rough.

Cassie opened the first scrapbook, realising then how tawdry it looked compared to the gold-encrusted ones he most probably had of his childhood. She had never been able to afford anything more than these cheap books, although she had promised herself once she was off the island and had some money to spare she was going to buy some proper albums.

'This is just after he was born,' she said, the rustle of the page turning over the only sound in the room.

Sebastian looked at the photo of his baby son lying on Cassie's chest, his tiny body still streaked with blood and the waxy protective covering of vernix from the womb. He hadn't cried since he was a small child but tears came to his eyes now and he had trouble seeing through them. The photograph blurred and he swallowed deeply.

'And this is when he was about two weeks old.' Cassie had turned another page, thankfully without looking up at him.

He looked at the prison-issue blanket covering his son and felt another blade of guilt slice him. Photo after photo had the same devastating effect on him. Pictures of Sam playing within the barbed-wire-enclosed prison, inmates all around, some of them looking less desirable than others.

Cassie reached for another scrapbook and showed him some clippings of Sam's hair and even the minuscule crescents of his fingernails. Sebastian reached out and touched the hair with his fingers; the dark curls could have been his when he was the same age. Emotion clogged his throat and he had to swallow again to clear it.

'I don't have many photos of when he was four,' Cassie said, still looking at the open book resting on Sebastian's thighs.

'Why not?' he asked.

She looked at him then. 'Because that was the year he was taken away from me,' she said with an embittered set to her mouth. 'The foster parents didn't think to take photographs for me. Why would they? I was just a prisoner.'

Sebastian began to understand then some of what she had gone through. He had missed out on five years of Sam's life but she, too, had missed out. She had lost six years of her young life, and a whole year of her son's with not even a photograph to comfort her. No wonder Sam was as shy as he was and so frightened of being separated from his mother. In each of the photos up until he turned three Sam was a happy, smiling little baby and toddler. It was only when Cassie showed him the remaining photos, including the ones up to date, that Sebastian could see what that year without his mother had done to Sam.

'Can I keep these for a few days?' he asked after a moment. 'I want to get some copies made.'

Cassie wasn't sure, but she thought she could see a hint of moisture in the darkness of his gaze. 'Of course,' she said. 'But please be careful with them. I've already lost a photo or two where the glue has come unstuck.'

'I will make sure they are handled with the utmost care,' he promised. 'Thank you for showing them to me. I cannot tell you what it has meant to me.'

Cassie compressed her lips, struggling to contain her own emotions. She got to her feet and, wrapping her arms around her body, faced him. 'I wanted to give him so much more,' she said. 'He deserved so much more. I'm so worried he will never get over it…you know, being taken away from me. That year he went to the foster home…' She released one of her hands to brush at her eyes and continued raggedly, 'I couldn't protect him. What if someone had hurt him? What if someone treated him roughly like my father did to me? I wasn't there for him, Sebastian. I wasn't there to protect him like no one was there to protect me…'

'Your father…' he swallowed over the word as he got to his feet '…abused you?'

Cassie couldn't speak. Tears were suddenly blocking her throat, burning, aching tears that were spilling from her eyes and rolling down her face.

Sebastian reached for her, enfolding her in his arms, stroking the back of her head, murmuring soothing, meaningless words to her as the storm of her emotions passed through her. He felt every quake of her body; every broken sob tore at him until his own eyes felt moist and his chest too tight to breathe.

'I'm sorry…'

She tried to push away from him but, although he allowed her some room, he didn't release her. He held her hands in his, his thumbs stroking over her fingers. 'Tell me everything, Cassie,' he said softly. 'You are safe now. No one is going to hurt you. I won't allow them to.'

She looked up at him, her chin trembling so like Sam's he felt another deep wave of emotion swamp him. He had missed out on so much but he was starting to realise most of the blame for that was his. He'd fallen into the same trap as everyone else, judging her without really knowing her. All the clues were there now that he had the benefit of hindsight. Each letter to the unsolvable crossword now in place, and his gut churned at what those letters spelt.

'He broke my arm.' The words tumbled out and once they had started Cassie couldn't seem to stop. 'He broke my arm when I was four years old. On the way to the hospital he told me if I said a word to anyone about how it had happened he would do much worse. He told me to tell everyone I had fallen off my bed. I was so frightened. It wasn't the first time he had hit me, far from it. He was always hitting me, but after that he toned it down a bit. It wouldn't do to have anyone pointing their finger at him, now, would it? He was a high-profile man who made a great show of how much he loved his difficult daughter.'

Sebastian kept on stroking her cold, lifeless hands. 'Oh, Cassie,' was all he could manage to say. 'Oh, my poor, Caz.'

She continued speaking in the same flat, emotionless tone. 'By the time I was a teenager I deliberately set out to shame him. I couldn't tell anyone about the physical abuse but I could still get at him that way, or so I thought. I guess I didn't stop to think about the consequences for my own life…'

'You were a child, for God's sake,' Sebastian said. 'A terrified child with no one you could turn to.'

'The night we broke up...' She paused, her face a picture of pain at the memory. 'I felt I had no choice. My father had so many times renewed his warning...I thought about going to the police, but he was best friends with the commissioner. He had powerful friends everywhere. I had nothing to fall back on but an already damaged reputation.'

Sebastian's frown deepened. 'So you made up a parcel of lies about sleeping around to put me off the scent?'

She nodded. 'I'm sorry... It must have hurt you but I couldn't think of what else to do. I couldn't see any future in our relationship. I was going to leave as soon as I turned eighteen in any case. My father saw my packed bags and...and that was it.'

'He attacked you?' His words were more of a statement than a question.

'Yes...I thought he was going to...to...' She screwed up her face as if she couldn't bear to say the word out loud.

Sebastian felt another sickening wave of nausea roll through him as he suddenly realised what word she was avoiding. He put his arms back around her, holding her close, trying to comfort a pain that could not be comforted. 'I'm so sorry.' The words seemed so inadequate and yet he kept saying them. 'I'm so very sorry. I wish I had been able to protect you. I wish I had known. I wish you had trusted me enough to tell me.'

He put her from him again, looking down at her reddened eyes. 'Did you ever consider telling someone during the trial about what you had suffered?' he asked. 'You could have shown them the X-rays from when you were a child. Surely someone would have listened.'

She gave him the bleakest of looks. 'I considered it a few times but I could see the disgust in everyone's eyes. I was a tramp, a rebellious little slut who had brought shame and disgrace on her poor, hard-working father. It was all so daunting.' She sighed and carried on sadly, 'When I found out I was pregnant I realised why I hadn't put up much of a fight. I was so tired and sick and so overwhelmed with it all I just sat there like an automaton without offering a word in my own defence.'

Sebastian gripped her hands. 'I will speak to my legal counsel,' he said. 'I'll have your name cleared. I will do everything within my power to see proper justice is served.'

'No,' she said, pulling out of his hold. 'I don't want to go through it all again. I just want to leave Aristo.'

Three beats of silence passed.

'You will not be leaving.'

Her eyes flared and a pulse began to beat at her throat. 'What do you mean I won't be leaving?' she asked.

'I will not allow you to take my son away,' he said. 'I have only just met him. I need time to get to know him before I announce to the press my intentions where he is concerned.'

Cassie tried to keep her panic contained but it bubbled up inside her. She could see his point of view, but she couldn't allow herself to be imprisoned again, even in such a gilded cage as the Karedes private villa. 'I will not allow you to keep me under house arrest,' she said, glaring at him. 'I want to be able to come and go as I see fit.'

'I am afraid that is impossible,' he said with an intransigent set to his features. 'I have to take every precaution that this situation is dealt with in the utmost secrecy.'

'It's all about you and your precious throne, isn't it?' she threw at him.

'It has nothing to do with the throne,' he ground out in frustration. 'I want to spend time with Sam without the paparazzi shoving cameras in his face. He's shy and—'

'So that's my fault, is it?' she asked. 'It's all because of the terrible mother he has—that's what you're thinking, isn't it?'

He shook his head at her, his eyes going upwards as if for patience from some higher source. 'I wasn't implying anything of the sort,' he said, lowering his voice. 'When the time is right I will have no hesitation in announcing to the people of Aristo you are the mother of my child.'

She gave him a churlish look. 'Yeah, well, I bet you won't do it until you have the paternity test results in your hands.'

He let out his breath in a whistling stream, a signal Cassie knew from past experience, he was nearing the end of his tether. 'What would you do if the tables were turned? Answer me, Cassie. What would you do?'

Cassie felt herself backing down. 'I—I would do the same...' she said, so low it was barely audible.

'Say it louder.'

She lifted her chin. 'You heard.'

'Say it louder,' he commanded again.

Cassie tightened her hands into fists, her anger rising up like lava, her voice rising along with it. 'I said I would do the same. I said I would do the same. I SAID I WOULD DO THE SAME.'

Sebastian captured her flailing hands before they could connect with his face as he supposed she intended. 'Stop it, Cassie. It's over...shhh, *agape mou,* it's over. I'm not fighting with you. I pushed you too far. I'm sorry, OK?'

She choked back a little sob. 'Don't you dare be nice to me... I can cope with you when you're not nice...'

He gave a rueful smile. 'That is the problem, isn't it? You are not used to people treating you with respect and consideration so you put up a prickly don't-mess-with-me front.'

She tried to avoid his gaze but he countered it by placing a gentle hand beneath her chin. 'Don't shut me out now, Caz,' he said. 'Not now. You can trust me. You do know that, don't you?'

Her throat went up and down. 'I'm not used to trusting anyone…'

'I know but that has to change. It is important you learn to trust me so that Sam bonds with me. He takes his cue from you, don't forget.'

Cassie searched his face. 'Can I trust you not to take him away from me?' she asked.

'I could ask you the very same question.'

'I won't take him away without you knowing about it.' Her gaze slipped to his mouth. 'I wasn't sure if you would see the likeness. I can see it, but then I am his mother.'

'I see it.'

Her eyes flicked back to his. 'Does that mean you don't question you are his father?'

'Cassie, the paternity test is not for me,' he said, taking her by the shoulders, his thumbs rubbing softly against her bare flesh. 'I know he is my son. I felt a connection when you gave me the painting he had done for me. I couldn't understand it at the time. I had this sudden urge to meet this child. It became my entire focus.'

'Were you really as shy as he is when you were small?' she asked.

He stroked a finger down the curve of her cheek. 'I was for a long time. I grew out of it eventually and I am sure he will too. You are a wonderful mother to him, Cassie. You remind me so much of my mother. I can see how much he adores you. You are his world.'

'I love him more than you will ever know,' she said softly. 'He's really my only reason for living. Before I found out I was carrying him I wanted to…to…'

He placed a fingertip against her lips. 'No, Cassie, don't

say it. I can't bear to hear you say it. I hate to think of what you went through. No wonder you were so angry at me for not responding to your letter.'

She gave him another searching look. 'So you believe now I sent one?'

'That is another thing I mulled over after you left my bed this morning,' he said. 'It is obvious my father must have ordered my mail to be screened. After all, he blocked Lissa from contacting you. There can be no other explanation.'

Cassie felt her shoulders start to relax. 'I'm glad you believe me… It's been so hard having no one on my side…'

His hands moved down the length of her arms to encircle her wrists. 'I am on your side now, Cassie, don't ever forget that. I will do whatever I can to make up for the past.'

She wanted to believe him, but she knew he couldn't have everything his way. What would be his final choice? It was too painful to even think about. All she knew was he couldn't have it all, and neither could she. They would both have to make a choice, but somehow she knew his was not going to include her, no matter how much she prayed it would.

CHAPTER ELEVEN

CASSIE spent the next few days watching as Sebastian spent time with Sam. It was so moving to see them together, their dark heads bent close together over a puzzle or a book or a painting they had done, their smiles so similar. Sam was starting to blossom, his confidence growing as each day passed. He clearly adored his father and Sebastian made no effort to hide his very deep love for his son.

Cassie tried not to let it concern her but Sebastian had not asked her to sleep with him again. Was he trying to distance himself from her? It was so hard to tell. When Sam was around he smiled and chatted with her as any set of normal parents would do, but as soon as Sam was in bed Sebastian excused himself from her company, citing business to see to, letters to write, phone calls to make, anything, it seemed, rather than spend time with her.

It made her feel so terribly insecure, especially when she had revealed her past to him. Had he found it too hard to cope with? Was that why he was avoiding her? He preferred to think of her as a sleep-around-slut he could lure back into an affair, but not as a young woman who had been mistreated and shown injustice all of her life.

'Now, young man,' Sebastian said as he picked up Sam

from the floor and set him on his shoulders. 'I am going to take you upstairs to bed where you should have been well over an hour ago.'

Sam giggled as he dug his hands into his father's hair to keep his balance. 'Will you take me down to the beach again tomorrow?' he asked.

'Yes, and I will even show you a cave where my brothers and sisters and I used to hide things, like buried treasure,' he said.

'Will it still be there?' Sam asked, bending round so he could look into his father's eyes.

Sebastian smiled. 'If it isn't we will bury some of our own,' he said. 'Now kiss Mummy goodnight.'

'I want you both to tuck me in,' Sam said.

Cassie met Sebastian's gaze for a brief moment before she looked up at Sam so high above her. 'Let Daddy tuck you in on his own, darling,' she said. 'I have done it so many times and he has got a lot of catching up to do.'

Sam's forehead began to wrinkle in a worried frown. 'But I want you there too, Mummy.'

Sebastian hauled Sam down off his shoulders and onto his hip instead. 'Of course Mummy can help me tuck you in,' he said. 'Now what story do you want me to read to you tonight?'

Sam looked up at him with big brown eyes. 'Mummy told me a story about a prince who found a shoe after a party and he searched to find the beautiful girl who had lost it. Do you know that story?'

Sebastian felt his chest tighten. 'Yes, I know that one. It's called *Cinderella*.'

'That's right!' Sam said excitedly. 'Isn't Daddy clever, Mummy? He knows the same stories you know.'

'Yes, he's very clever, darling,' she said, her cheeks flushing slightly.

A few minutes later Sebastian rose from where he had

been sitting on his son's bed. Sam was fast asleep, his breathing deep and even, his angelic face a picture of contentment.

He watched as Cassie leaned over and pressed a soft kiss to Sam's forehead, her fingers brushing the hair back off his face, the look of love on her face making him feel another deep pang of regret for all she had gone through.

'Have you got a minute to have a chat?' he asked once they had both left Sam's room.

She gave him an ironic look. 'I'm the one with all the time on my hands, Sebastian,' she said with a touch of resentment. 'You're the one who is always too busy.'

'You are feeling neglected,' Sebastian said, blowing out a sigh. 'I am sorry, but being away from the palace like this means I have things to see to each night. When I've come to your room you have always been asleep. I didn't want to disturb you.'

Her forehead creased. 'You came to my room?'

He gave her a wry smile. 'You should not sound so surprised, Cassie. I thought I had made it clear how much I want you.'

She lowered her gaze a fraction. 'Yes, but I thought you had changed your mind…or something…'

He placed his hands at her waist. 'That is the whole trouble, Cassie,' he said. 'I want what I cannot have.'

She looked up at him, her eyes uncertain. 'I'm not asking for for ever, Sebastian.'

His chest rose and fell on another sigh. 'I know, and that is what concerns me the most,' he said. 'You and Sam deserve for ever. You both deserve the happiness that has been stolen from you.'

Cassie could see the struggle he was having played out on his face. He had deep shadows under his eyes as if he had not slept at all over the last few nights. She wanted to tell him how much she loved him but knew it would only make his decision all the harder to make. He was already carrying a load of guilt and was doing everything in his power to make it up to Sam. 'You are a fantastic father,' she said softly. 'Sam loves you so much.'

'I love him too,' he said, looking into her eyes. 'I cannot tell you how much.'

'I know how much,' she said. 'I feel that way too.'

His hands moved from her waist. 'I have something to show you,' he said. 'They arrived this afternoon.'

Cassie followed him downstairs to his study where he showed her how he had had all the photographs of Sam copied and reset into four leather-bound albums, each one with the gold crest of the Karedes family on the cover. She couldn't speak for a moment; she sat silently tracing her fingertip over the royal crest, wondering if this was part of the removal process. He was making the disparity of their lives and background all the more apparent. He was showing her where Sam belonged, where she could never follow.

'What do you think?' he asked.

She brought her gaze up to his. 'I think you are systematically trying to nudge me out of his life, that's what I think.'

His brows came together. 'What are you talking about? I had those done for you. I have another set made for myself.'

She got to her feet and crossed her arms over her chest. 'What have you done with the originals?'

'I threw them out,' he said. 'They were falling apart in any case.'

Cassie glared at him in fury. 'You threw them out? Is that what you're telling me? You threw my scrapbooks out?'

'Cassie, what is all the fuss about?' he asked. 'You would surely have replaced them yourself when you found the time.'

'You had no right to throw away what was mine,' she said, fighting back tears. 'I had to work hard to pay for those books. I had to barter with food and privileges to pay for them and now you've tossed them out as if they're worth nothing. Do you have any idea how that makes me feel?'

He came over to where she was standing. 'I think I am starting to get a sense of what you are feeling,' he said gently. 'You had so little to give Sam but you gave him everything you could. Those scrapbooks represented some of the sacrifices you had been forced to make. I am sorry, Cassie. I will call Stefanos and have him return them to you. It was wrong of me to assume they were not valuable to you.'

Cassie could feel her defences crumbling. Tears she had sworn she was not going to allow to fall were already falling, one by one, but before she could brush them away with her hands Sebastian got there first. With a touch so gentle he blotted each tear with the pad of his thumbs.

'I'm sorry,' she said. 'I shouldn't have been so touchy about it.'

His eyes darkened as they held hers. 'I do not know how to make it up to you, for all you have lost, for all that I could have prevented if I had taken the time to get to know you. I have been doing some research on your father. He had friends in so many high places it was no wonder you felt you had no one to go to. I had my aide request the medical records of when you were admitted to the hospital when you were four, and there was no record of you ever being admitted.'

Cassie felt her shoulders go down. 'I didn't stand a chance, did I?'

'I will get justice for you, Cassie,' he said, pulling her closer. 'I will leave no stone unturned until I do.'

Cassie was standing too close to him to be able to ignore the pulse of his body, and the thin layer of her clothes that shielded her form couldn't possibly disguise her own response to his nearness. She ran her tongue over the dryness of her lips;

her breathing going out of time, her heart tripping as his head slowly came down...

The press of his lips against hers was gentle at first, but as soon as he stroked his tongue across the seam of her lips everything changed. Passion flared like a combustible fuel exposed to a lighted taper. It streaked along Cassie's veins, thundering in her ears and pooling in her belly like liquid fire. She felt the hard probe of his body against the flimsy barrier of her gown, the intimate closeness making it all that harder to move away. His mouth was burning hot, his tongue insistent and determined as it conquered hers.

He backed her towards the sofa, his muscled thighs rubbing along hers with every heart-stopping step. She felt the cushions at the back of her knees and went down with barely a whimper, her mouth locked on his.

His hands peeled away the spaghetti-thin shoulder straps on her sundress, his mouth moving from hers to blaze down past her shoulders to her breasts. She bit back a gasp as the heated moistness of his mouth closed over her nipple, the sexy scrape of his teeth sending arrows of delight to her already-curling toes. She felt her body secretly preparing for him, the on-off pulse of her inner muscles making her wild to feel him deep and hard within her.

His mouth moved farther down her body, giving her small niplike kisses that sent her senses spinning even further out of control. She was writhing beneath his solid weight, desperate to get closer, her hands tearing at his clothes so she could feel him skin on skin.

He captured her hands and held them above her head, his dark eyes glinting with rampant desire. 'Don't be so impatient, *agape mou,*' he teased playfully. 'I am getting to that.'

'I want you *now,*' she said, arching up against him. 'You're taking too long.'

'It is all the better for waiting, Cassie,' he said. 'Can you feel it building and building?'

Cassie could and it was driving her crazy. 'I want to touch you,' she said. 'Let me go so I can touch you properly.'

His eyes burned into hers for a heady moment before he released her hands. 'Touch me all you like, Cassie,' he said, and shrugged himself out of his shirt.

Cassie needed no other inducement. She had his belt off and his waistband undone within seconds, her fingers enclosing him with just the right amount of tension to make him cut back a groan of pleasure. She moved her hand up and down, watching as he fought to keep control.

When he tried to stop her she pushed his hand away, and, giving him a sultry look, bent her mouth to him. She felt him shudder as she took the first strong suck, a whole-body shudder that sent shivers of vicarious pleasure up and down her spine. The tension in his body was electrifying; she could feel it building to explosion point. She could taste him, that salt and musk combination that was as erotic as it was irresistible.

'Enough, oh, dear God in heaven, enough,' he groaned and pulled out.

Cassie ran the point of her tongue over her lips, knowing it would drive him wild. 'Am I going too fast for you?' she asked with an arch look.

'Not fast enough,' he growled, and pressed her back down with his weight coming over her.

Cassie shivered as he pulled her dress off her body with a total disregard for the delicate fabric. She heard it tear but was too far gone to fully register it. He nudged her thighs apart, the first stablike thrust of his body ricocheting through her as he drove home to the hilt. He set a fast pace, but she delighted in every exhilarating second of it, her body on fire as her senses climbed to the summit of human pleasure. Every nerve was screaming for release, her legs were quivering, her back arching and her breathing choppy and uneven as he drove her to the edge time and time again, only to pull back at the last teetering moment.

'Don't make me beg,' she panted against his moist mouth.

'I want you to beg,' he said against her lips. 'I want you to scream at me to give you what you want.'

She bit at him, a playful puppy bite. 'Someone might hear us,' she said.

'I don't give a damn who hears us,' he said. 'Tell me what you want, Cassie.'

'I want you to make me come,' she said, pulling his head back down to hers.

He crushed her mouth beneath his, his body hard and urgent in hers as one of his hands went between their bodies to caress the swollen centre of her desire. Cassie bit back a cry as she began to soar, each smashing wave of release making her body convulse around him. She sobbed her way through it, the power of it unlike anything she had ever felt before.

He came close behind, his body tensing for the final plunge, every muscle under her fingertips bunching before he emptied himself.

Cassie let her hands skate over his back and shoulders in the aftermath, her heart still hammering, her breathing just as erratic as his. It was times like this she could almost imagine a different life for herself, a life where she would wake up each morning next to Sebastian, his legs entwined with hers, the essence of him still hot and wet between her thighs…

Her heart suddenly gave a sideways lurch. 'Oh, no…'

Sebastian eased himself off her. 'What's wrong, Cassie? Did I hurt you? Was I too rough?'

She gave him a wide-eyed look of alarm. 'You didn't use a condom.'

'I know,' he said with a rueful grimace. 'But I'm all clear, so don't worry.'

Cassie searched for her dress and underwear, trying not to let her panic take too many fast strides. 'I can't believe you didn't use a condom,' she said, tossing aside the sofa cushions.

'Cassie, I told you I won't give you anything.'

'No,' she said, turning her back on him as she reached for her dress lying on the floor. 'Or at least nothing you haven't already given me in the past.'

Sebastian didn't take in what she had said. He stared at the jagged white scar near her tailbone for what seemed like endless seconds. 'How long have you had that scar?' he asked.

He saw her stiffen before she turned to face him. 'What scar?'

He got to his feet and came over to where she was standing. 'I think you know what I am talking about. I've never seen it before.'

'Yes, well, I've never been totally naked with you before,' she said, flashing her green eyes at him in irritation.

He placed his hands on her shoulders to stop her from spinning away. 'You don't have to cover up for him now, Cassie,' he said in as gentle a tone as he could. 'If your father did that to you then you have no reason not to tell me.'

He felt the tremble of her body under his hands and his heart contracted when he saw fresh tears well in her eyes. 'Look, it was a long time ago and I'd rather just forget about it,' she said.

'How long?'

She bit her lip. 'The night I got home from breaking off things with you…'

Sebastian closed his eyes for a moment before drawing her close, his hands touching her as if she were a fragile work of art, his gut wrenching all over again as his fingers traced over the ribbed flesh of her back. 'I know it is of no comfort, but if you had told me it would have been me in that jail, not you,' he said. 'I would have killed him for what he has done to you. I swear to God I would have torn him from limb to limb.'

'I wouldn't have wanted you to do that,' she said, looking up at him.

Sebastian brought one of her hands to his mouth and brushed his lips over the back of her knuckles. 'Come with me upstairs,' he said. 'I want to spend tonight holding you in my arms.'

She looked as if she was going to say no, but then she gave him a smile tinged with sadness. 'I guess we should make the most of the time we have left…'

Sebastian didn't want to think about how each day was slipping through his fingers like fine grains of sand. All he could hope for was a few more days to keep Sam and Cassie close while he sorted through his options. Everything had happened so quickly and he was still coming to terms with it all. Not just Sam's existence but how his feelings for Cassie were rising up to the surface after years of being shoved down.

He led her upstairs to his bedroom, closing the door softly behind them. 'I was thinking about having a shower,' he said. 'Would you like to join me?'

'It's all right,' she said, perching on the edge of his bed, not quite meeting his eyes. 'I'll wait until you're finished and then have one.'

It struck him then, how shy she was. No doubt ashamed of how disfigured her body was by that horrible scar. His gut clenched all over again at what she had suffered at that madman's hands. 'No,' he said, keeping his voice steady but only just. 'You go first. I have a couple of calls to make in any case.'

When he came back she was lying in amongst his pillows, looking small and fragile and uncertain. He came over to her and, picking up one of her hands, brought it up to his mouth, kissing her palm and then each of her fingers in turn. 'I just checked on Sam,' he said. 'He was fast asleep.'

Sebastian leaned forward and pressed a soft kiss to her forehead. 'I am going to have a quick shower. Don't go to sleep on me now, will you, *agape mou?*'

She gave him a small smile but there was still that haunting air of sadness in her green eyes. 'I won't.'

Cassie waited for him, her heart feeling like an engine in her chest when he came back out of the bathroom, dressed in nothing but a towel tied loosely at his hips. He was so magnificently built, so commandingly male. He dropped the towel and turned back the sheets to slip in beside her, taking her in his arms and holding her close for a long time without speaking.

She listened to his breathing, heard his heartbeat pounding against her cheek, storing away the clean male scent of him to comfort her in the lonely years to come.

She had thought he had fallen asleep but slowly his hands began to move over her, slow, gentle caressing movements, a touch that was almost reverent.

'Your skin feels like silk,' he breathed against her ear.

She shivered as his mouth sealed hers in a kiss of passionate possession, his tongue meeting hers in a slow tango that stirred her deeply.

He lifted his mouth off hers to kiss each of her breasts, taking his time, his tongue rolling and licking and tasting her until her back was arching off the bed.

He moved down her body, dipping into the cave of her belly button before going to the secret heart of her, tasting her, teasing her until she was gasping her way through a shattering release.

Cassie wanted to pleasure him but he seemed in no hurry to have her do anything but lie there and have him worship her body. He kept pushing her hands away, kissing her into silence, stroking all of her tension away with the glide of his hands.

At one point he turned her over. She resisted at first but he kissed away her doubts and gently turned her onto her stomach. She felt each and every kiss as he travelled down the length of her spine, his lips lingering over her scar, as if he wanted to take away the pain of the memories it had scored on her brain, much less her skin.

When he turned her back over he could see the tears in her eyes and dabbed them away with the edge of the sheet. 'I wish I could make the past go away for you, Cassie,' he said. 'I want to bring this out in the open, to tell the people of this island how unjustly you were treated.'

She moved out of his embrace. 'It's over and I need to move on for Sam's sake. I don't want him to know about any of this, that's why I want to get right away where no one knows me. He's already heard too much.'

'Cassie, I can't allow you to leave Aristo until I think it is appropriate,' he said with a frown. 'Surely you under-stand that?'

'I do understand the situation you are in and I am making no demands on you other than to give me my freedom.'

His eyes warred with hers for several tense seconds. 'I am not going to let you walk away, Cassie. If I have to lock every door you are behind, I will do it.'

Cassie swung away in fury, ripping the sheet off the bed to cover herself. 'I suppose not using a condom downstairs was part of your insurance policy, was it?' she bit out bitterly.

'What?'

She turned back to look at him. 'I'm not on the pill, Sebastian, so you had better start crossing your fingers and hope and pray that lightning doesn't strike in the same place twice.'

Sebastian stared at her for a stunned moment or two. 'Do you think it's possible?' he finally managed to croak out. 'Where are you in your cycle?'

'There is never a safe time,' she said. 'If I fell pregnant on the pill, God only knows how quickly I will do so without it.'

He raked a hand through his hair. 'I need some time to think about this…'

'Why don't you get back to me in, say, six years?' she said with an embittered look.

He set his mouth. 'I know I probably more than deserve that, Cassie, but I did not intend for you to be put in such a compromising situation. Not the first time and certainly not now.'

'Do you think I wanted this to happen all over again?' she asked. 'You were the one to suggest we rake over the coals of the past by sleeping together again.'

He knew she was right. He had pressured her into an affair that could only have one outcome.

'I can say no to anyone else but you,' she said. 'I hate you for it.'

He moved over to her, taking her by the upper arms, his hold firm but gentle. 'I know you hate me, Caz. I hate myself, to tell you the truth. But hate is going to get us nowhere. It is important for Sam that he sees us getting along as any other mature and sensible couple would do.'

'But we're not a couple,' she said, wriggling out of his hold. 'We never have been and we never will be.'

Sebastian couldn't read her expression, which frustrated him more than he wanted to admit. What was she implying? That she wanted something more permanent, had *always* wanted something more lasting? His mind whirled as he thought about all the obstacles they would face if he presented her to the public as his chosen partner. And there was Sam to consider. How would he cope with suddenly being in the spotlight? Sebastian knew the people of Aristo would never accept Cassie Kyriakis as their queen. Even if he hired every top lawyer to clear her name he wasn't sure if it would achieve much. People formed their own opinions and were loath to change them, even if a solid case was put before them.

As to his own feelings, well, Sebastian was still trying to sort it all out in his head. He had been so determined to right the wrongs of the past with a short-term affair with her, but it had blown up in his face upon finding out about Sam, not to mention the harrowing details of Cassie's home life. The love he had felt for her six years ago had been locked away— he had thought for ever. He had duties to face, responsibilities and expectations he had been schooled and prepared for all his life. Walking away from all that was rightly his and expected of him by the people of Aristo was not something to be taken lightly.

And there was his brother Alex to consider. He and his wife Maria were expecting the birth of their first child in a day or two. Alex had always expressed his reluctance to take up the throne. How would he feel if Sebastian gave him no other choice?

'Cassie, it is not my intention to imprison you, anything but. You will be safe here without the press hounding you. Believe me that is my only motivation, to keep you and Sam safe.'

'All right,' she said on an expelled breath. 'You've got two weeks but that's all.'

CHAPTER TWELVE

'DADDY says I can have a real paint set and brushes and a…a…*weasel* all to myself!' Sam announced proudly as he came running towards Cassie one morning four days later.

'Easel,' she said as she bent down to kiss his forehead. 'It's called an easel. A weasel is a small furry animal.'

'Oh…' Sam went on excitedly. 'I've got a new tip truck and a kite Daddy and me are going to use on the beach and Daddy promised me I can have a camera all of my own when I am six.'

Cassie forced a smile in spite of her inner turmoil. How could she tell Sam this week of indulgence was soon to end? She had no doubt Sebastian would continue contact with his son; he had made that very clear every night they had spent together. In such a short time he had established a loving relationship with Sam that had many times brought tears to her eyes. It made what she had missed out on during her childhood all the more painfully apparent. But in spite of the tenderness and passion they had shared night after night Sebastian had mentioned nothing about her place in his life. Cassie knew Sam would always be known as the king's love-child, a mistake from his past, the one blemish he couldn't erase. And as the child's mother she would be shunted sideways; there would be no place for her once he stepped up to the throne.

'Daddy's going to have breakfast with me,' Sam said. 'I'm going to have pancakes. He said I could have anything I wanted.'

'Darling…' Cassie took his hands in hers. 'I don't think it's—'

'It's all right,' Sebastian said from just behind her. 'I'll deal with this.'

Something about his demeanour alerted her to an undercurrent of tension. He had brought it into the room with him, like a blast of cold air when someone opened a door leading into a warm room.

He crouched in front of Sam. 'Sam, Mummy and I have some things to discuss. Eleni will see to your breakfast this morning but I promise I will have lunch with you instead.'

'What sort of things do you have to talk about?' Sam asked with a worried look between his parents. 'I'm not going back to the orphanage, am I? I don't want to go back. I like being with you, Daddy, and Mummy does too, don't you, Mummy?'

Cassie forced her mouth to smile in response. 'I love being anywhere you are, darling.'

'I know you like being here, Sam,' Sebastian said after glancing for a moment at Cassie. 'I love having you here with me.'

'Can I stay for ever?' Sam asked with hope shining brightly in his chocolate-brown eyes. 'I love you. I'll be very good. I promise. I won't wet my pants any more. I'll try really hard. Really, *really* hard.'

Sebastian felt his heart lodge itself halfway up his throat so he could barely speak. 'Sam, you don't have to do anything but be yourself,' he said. 'I love you just the way you are.'

'So I'm not going to be sent away?' Sam asked.

Sebastian could feel the tension coming off Cassie standing at his left shoulder. 'Here is Eleni now. I will come back for you later.'

Cassie watched as Sam scampered off towards Eleni before she turned to face Sebastian. 'Nice one, Karedes,' she sniped at him. 'How to bribe a little kid away from its mother in just over a week. God, you make me sick.'

A flicker of anger passed through his dark eyes as they clashed with hers. 'I am doing no such thing. Come into the study out of the hearing of the staff.'

'I know what you're doing,' she said as she trotted to keep up with his long strides. 'You're making Sam so dependent on you he won't even notice when I'm gone. That's what your plan is, isn't it? To get me out of the picture as soon as you can. You're showering him with toys and giving him choices and opportunities I could never give him. It will make him think I don't love him the way you supposedly do.'

He frowned down at her. 'You consider what I feel for Sam is not genuine?'

She captured her lip between her teeth. 'No…no, I'm not saying that… I know you love him and he loves you.'

'How could I not love him?' he asked, holding open the study door for her to pass through. 'He is so engaging and so innocent I want to protect him as much as possible. He has been through so much for one so young. I am doing what I can to make it up to him.'

'I don't want him to be hurt,' she said. 'He doesn't really understand the circumstances of your life. He thinks things will continue as they are, but they can't and you need to prepare him for it.'

He closed the study door and, moving across the room, picked up a newspaper. 'If you did not want to see Sam hurt, then why on earth did you do this?' he asked, handing her the paper.

Cassie stared down at the headlines. There was a photograph of Sam on the front page with: FUTURE KING'S LOVE-CHILD REVEALED BY EX-PRISONER CASSIE KYRIAKIS emblazoned beneath. She looked up at Sebastian's glittering gaze. 'You think *I'm* responsible for this?' she choked.

He folded his arms, one ankle crossing over the other as he leaned back against his desk in an accusatory manner. 'Don't play games with me, Cassie. I know, in spite of what we have shared over the last couple of weeks, deep down you have always wanted to get back at me for how I let you down. But using Sam as a pawn is taking things a little too far. The press have gone wild with this. There are camera crews and television vans at the gate as we speak.'

Cassie took an uneven swallow. 'I didn't speak to anyone… How can you think I would do something like this?'

'Have you spoken to your flatmate in the last couple of days?'

Cassie suddenly remembered the call she had received from Angelica a couple of days ago. Angelica had heard rumours circulating and had wanted to know what was going on. Cassie had confessed all and had sworn her to silence, trusting her implicitly to keep Sam's paternity a secret.

'Cassie?' Sebastian's voice was brittle. 'Have you spoken to Angelica about this?'

'Yes, but she would never—'

He let out a stiff curse. 'And you trusted that junkie?' he asked incredulously.

She set her mouth. 'Yes, I do, as a matter of fact. I trust her more than I've ever trusted anyone.'

His eyes remained hard. 'Do you recognise the photo?'

She looked at it again. 'Yes…yes, I do,' she said. 'It's one of the ones I lost somewhere.'

He hooked one dark brow upwards. 'Lost or sold to the press via your drugged-up flatmate?'

She put the newspaper down with an unsteady hand. 'Angelica is not a drugged-up junkie. She is my best friend— she stood by me when no one else could give a toss.'

'That's what this is about, isn't it?' He waved the paper in her face. 'I didn't stand up for you when you needed me to so this is payback time.'

'How could you possibly think I would betray you or Sam in such a way?' Cassie asked, tears starting to spring to her eyes as she looked deeply into his. 'I love you both too much to ever do that.'

He went very still, his eyes losing some of their hardness. 'You love me?' he asked huskily.

Cassie pressed her lips together. 'I'm sorry… I shouldn't have let that slip out. I don't want to make things any more complicated than they already are.'

He pushed himself away from the table. 'Is this a new thing or an old thing?'

'Me loving you?' she asked, sweeping her tongue over her dry lips uncertainly.

He nodded without speaking, but she saw his throat rising and falling over a swallow, as if her confession had stunned him, but he was trying to conceal how much.

She twisted her hands together. 'It's an old thing…six years to be exact…I have always loved you, Seb.'

The silence hung like an axe over Cassie's head. She held her breath, wondering what he was going to say in response or if he was going to try and ignore her declaration of love because of the circumstances that made it impossible for them to ever be together.

'Remember I said the first night we spent together I had a photograph of you that you hadn't seen?' he said in a tone that had softened considerably.

'Yes…I forgot to ask you to show it to me,' she said, and felt her cheeks grow warm as she remembered why she hadn't thought to ask. She had been too distracted making love with him to think of anything but the pleasure he had made her feel.

He walked over to a table where a frame was sitting next to a vase of flowers. He came back over and handed her the frame and she looked down at it for a long time without speaking. It was a side-on shot of her, standing looking out to sea close to sunset, some strands of her long hair blowing across her face. Cassie could remember the exact day. It was two days before her father's death. She had gone down to the shore after a particularly nasty argument with him. He had raged at her over something insignificant and petty, slapping her across the face, not hard enough to leave a mark but enough to make her skin burn for hours afterwards. Once he had gone upstairs to drink himself into oblivion, as had become his habit, she had slipped out to walk along the beach, knowing if she stayed out long enough he would be asleep by the time she got back.

She had walked along the shore, stopping now and again to look out to sea, agonising over what to do about her relationship with Sebastian. How ironic he had captured the very moment she had decided to end their affair. She had stood there, mentally rehearsing what she was going to say to him, word by word, over and over until she had felt confident enough to convince him every lie was true.

Cassie had known one of Sebastian's hobbies was photography. She had seen several shots Sebastian had taken in the past, but there was something about this photograph that showed how talented he really was. He had not only captured a moment in time, he had captured a mood and made it almost tangible.

Cassie felt tears stinging at the backs of her eyes for how much her life had changed in the space of those next two days. She had been so young, so lost and alone in spite of all the people she had surrounded herself with.

To conceal her emotions she handed him back the frame with a stiff smile. 'You should have told me you were taking it,' she said. 'I would have fixed my hair at the very least.'

He looked at the photograph for a moment before putting it aside. 'I was about to call out to you but then I stopped. I decided to capture your image without you knowing you were being photographed.'

'Why did you keep it?' Cassie asked after a tiny pause.

His dark eyes meshed with hers. 'Have you ever had an item of clothing in your wardrobe you don't wear any more but still don't feel quite ready to discard it?'

She gave him an ironic look. 'I am quite sure you are not the one in your household to sort through your socks and underwear drawer. You have numerous servants who do that for you.'

His smile was a little crooked. 'Yes, perhaps you are right. There are not many things I do for myself these days.'

'Including choosing a wife?' Cassie wished she hadn't let it slip out, for she was sure she sounded as jealous as she felt.

He held her gaze for an interminable moment. 'As future King I am expected to marry and marry well. But I will have no one else make the final choice for me.'

A silence began to thicken the air.

'I have a meeting with my brother Alex later this morning back at the palace,' Sebastian said. 'In time I will be making my own statement to the press about Sam.'

Her eyes flared in alarm. 'What?'

His mouth was set in a determined line. 'I want to present Sam as my son. I don't want him hidden away as if I am ashamed of him. I am not. He is my flesh and blood.'

'But what about what I want?' she said. 'Do you have any idea of what the press will do to me? They'll crucify me all over again. I know they will. Look at what they have already said. How can I stop Sam hearing that stuff about me?'

'I realise the implications for you, Cassie, and I will do my best to defend you.'

'You weren't too keen on defending me a few minutes

ago,' she threw back. 'You were accusing me of selling this scandal to the press. It just shows how little you know me.'

'I apologise for jumping to conclusions,' Sebastian said. 'I didn't think it through logically. You are the last person to have spoken to the press. My absence from the palace has no doubt added to the speculation along with the issue of the missing diamond.'

'What missing diamond?'

Sebastian waited a beat before telling her. She had a right to know what he had been facing over the last few months. He could trust her to keep it quiet, of that he was now sure. Her love for him was something he had not been expecting, although it warmed him to the very core of his being. He just wanted a few more days to give Alex time to think over the proposition he had put before him.

'So can't you be King without the diamond?' she asked once he had finished.

'The coronation is still being planned, but there is no guarantee the diamond will be located in time,' he said. 'This must go no further than these four walls, Cassie.'

'You can trust me, Sebastian.'

He bent down and brushed his mouth against hers. 'I know I can, *agape mou*,' he said, and, touching her briefly on the curve of her cheek, added gently, 'I just wish I had trusted you from the beginning.'

The news about Sebastian's love-child went on for several days, which rather ironically made Cassie glad he had insisted she stay at Kionia with Sam. She had hardly seen Sebastian over the last four days; he had come back late at night, spending long hours in his study or pacing the floor of his room. She had wanted to go to him so many times but felt if he wanted to be with her he would have said so by now. In spite of her confession of love, he had not spoken of his own feelings. She was left in limbo, wishing and hoping for something that deep down she knew could never be.

The day of her parole came and she came to a decision. She called Angelica, who agreed to meet her and Sam at the front gates of the hideaway just as the guards were changing shifts. It was a risky move, but Cassie felt if she didn't leave now it would make it all the more difficult for Sam in the long run. She packed the things she had brought plus as much of what Sebastian had given Sam as he could fit into two bags.

While Eleni was occupied elsewhere, Cassie carried the bags downstairs, but just as she was about to store them in a cupboard the front door opened and Sebastian came in.

His eyes went to the bags in her hands. 'What are you doing?' he asked with a heavy frown.

She put the bags down and faced him determinedly. 'I am leaving with Sam,' she said. 'Nothing you say will stop me. I have made up my mind. My parole is up. I am a free woman.'

'You were going to just walk out without saying goodbye?' he asked in a flintlike tone. 'You weren't even going to let me speak to Sam?'

Cassie could feel the anger coming off him but stood her ground. 'You've barely seen him for the last few days,' she said. 'I thought it best to get out before he becomes even more attached to you.'

'You thought it best to take my son away from me?' he barked at her. 'How could you think that was the best thing for Sam, or even me for that matter?'

'We don't belong in your life,' Cassie said, holding back tears. 'The press have gone on and on about my background. I can't bear it any more. I can't even look at the paper now without feeling sick to my stomach.'

'So you haven't seen today's paper?'

She shook her head. 'No…no, I haven't…'

'There's an exclusive interview with someone from the orphanage called Spiro who claims he slept with you several times.'

Cassie felt her despair hit an all-time low. 'And you believed him?'

He let out a gust of breath after a tense moment. 'Of course I don't believe him. I have reason to believe he is the one behind the press leak.'

'Thank you for believing me,' Cassie said, blinking back tears. 'I can't tell you how much that means to me. No matter what happens I won't let Sam forget how wonderful you have been to me.'

He gave her an unreadable look as he unfolded the newspaper again. 'Since you haven't read the rest of the news I think you should know my younger brother Alex and his wife Maria had a baby girl late last night,' he said. 'They have called her Alexandria.'

'Oh, that's lovely news,' she said. 'I hope everything went well with the delivery.'

He drew in a breath as he tossed the paper to one side. 'Yes, it all went very well. Alex was over the moon, raving about the birth, how he cut the cord and held his daughter before anyone else touched her. It was obviously a very moving experience for him, and of course for Maria.'

Cassie bit down on her lip as she saw the raw emotion on his face. Even though she had shown him all the photos she had of Sam she knew it would never make up for him not being there as his brother had been for his wife for the birth of their tiny daughter. She even wondered if he truly had forgiven her for not trying harder to contact him about the pregnancy. Although he had shown amazing compassion over what she had suffered at the hands of her father, there was a part of her that suspected Sebastian had yet to process his feelings about having a love-child to a woman his people saw as not fit to stand by his side as his future queen.

'I have to leave, Sebastian,' she said into the creaking silence. 'Surely you see that? This will all blow over once Sam and I are off the island. It's the best way—the *only* way. If you truly love Sam then you will let me take him away where he can't be hurt by all the speculation and innuendo.'

Sebastian knew she was right about Sam. He was far too young and vulnerable to cope with the press, but how could he let his little son go? He had only just started to get to know him. There was so much he didn't know and would never know if he was not in close contact with his little boy. He felt as if he were being torn in two. Whatever decision he made was going to affect someone adversely.

And then there was Cassie. How could he let her leave now that he knew what he felt for her, what he had always felt for her? The last couple of weeks had shown him how much he had misjudged her. His guilt was like a yoke about his shoulders; he couldn't shake it off no matter what she said to exonerate him. There had been so little time to right the wrongs of the past, if indeed they ever could be righted.

He had already spoken to his legal advisors about clearing Cassie's name, but they had not been overwhelmingly positive. They had argued that it would look as if the Prince Regent of Aristo was manipulating the system in order to whitewash his mistress. Sebastian recognised it was politically sensitive, but he was more concerned about doing the right thing by Cassie and Sam. But perhaps the right thing *was* to let them leave Aristo, at least until the scandal died down a bit.

'All right,' he said, releasing a jagged sigh. 'I will let you and Sam go, but I must insist you keep me informed at all times of where you are. I will see that you are both provided for, and I would like to see Sam when it can be arranged. I would also like to spend some time with him before you leave in the morning.'

'Of course,' Cassie said, swallowing against a groundswell of emotion. He was letting them go. He had made his choice and it did not include her and Sam. But then why was she so heart-wrenchingly disappointed? Hadn't she always known she and Sebastian were never going to be together? She had known it from the very first time they had met six years ago. Sam's existence didn't change anything—why should it?

Sebastian had responsibilities that went back for centuries. Royal courts had dealt with this sort of situation many times before. The mistress and child were taken care of well out of the eye of the public, and in time completely forgotten.

Sebastian came up to her and, bending down, pressed his mouth to hers in a soft kiss that tasted to Cassie of goodbye. Her lips clung to his for a brief moment, as if trying to delay the final moment of separation.

She stood back from him and gave him a wry look. 'I guess it would be rather tacky to say at this point, thanks for the memories.'

The movement of his lips was nowhere near a smile, more of a grimace of regret. 'Thank you for my son,' he said in a deep, rough tone as he touched her on the cheek in a finger-tip caress.

Cassie knew if she didn't move away now she would crack. She pulled her shoulders back and pasted a smile on her face. 'Thank you for my freedom,' she said, and turned and walked up the stairs.

CHAPTER THIRTEEN

CASSIE was besieged by the press on her way to the ferry with Sam the next morning. Sam was already in tears, not quite understanding what was going on. Sebastian had spent some time with him earlier, but he had left before Cassie could see him one last time. Eleni had said he had been called away to something urgent at the palace, but Cassie had wondered if the old woman had been told to say that so Sebastian could avoid saying goodbye.

'But I don't want to leave Daddy,' Sam wailed as she tugged him along the gangplank to board the passenger ferry.

'Sweetie, it's just not possible to stay here,' she said, fighting back tears of her own at some of the vicious insults still being thrown at her from the wharf.

Cassie kept her head down as she showed their boarding passes to the ticket officer, her hands shaking so much the passes rattled like leaves in a stiff breeze.

Finally they were on their way, and Sam out of sheer exhaustion fell asleep on her lap, his face still blotchy from crying. Cassie sat stroking his hair, tears rolling down her cheeks as the island began to shrink as the ferry cut through the choppy water.

'Dhespinis Kyriakis?' A woman of about thirty seemed to

come out of nowhere. 'Do you mind if I sit down next to you and your little boy?'

Cassie could hardly say no as the seat next to her was vacant; in fact it was the only vacant one on that side of the ferry. 'If you like,' she said, and cuddled Sam closer.

'I heard what people were saying back there on the wharf,' the woman said after a moment.

Cassie tightened her mouth as she looked at the woman. 'If you have something to add to what has already been said, then forget it. I have heard it all before.'

'I am not here to insult you,' the woman said. 'I am here because I want to set the record straight. You see…I knew your father.'

Something about the woman's grim tone made Cassie's eyes widen in interest. 'You…you did?'

'I used to work for him ten years ago,' she said. 'He continually harassed me, threatened me and even on one occasion physically assaulted me, but every time I tried to report it, he circumvented it by smearing my reputation by spreading rumours around the council chambers. I was too young and inexperienced to know how to handle it, so in the end I left. It took me years before I found my feet again. I've only been working as a journalist in London for the last couple of years.'

Cassie felt her back stiffen. 'A journalist?'

'Please don't be worried,' the woman said. 'I was visiting relatives on Calista and heard about the Prince Regent's love-child. Your name leapt off the page. I knew when I read you had been imprisoned for the manslaughter of your father that there had to be more to it than that. I wanted to meet you, to interview you so you can tell your side of the story so you can receive the justice you have so far been denied. I will back you up and by doing so receive the justice I, too, was denied all those years ago.'

Cassie chewed at her lip. Should she do it, for Sam's sake if not her own? After all, he would be the one who had to live with the stigma of having an ex-prisoner as his mother. If she could clear her name it would be one step in the long road to recovering her life. And not just her life, but this young woman's who had also suffered at her father's hands. 'I'm not sure where to begin...' she said.

The young woman offered her hand. 'My name is Alexia and I always think the best place to start is at the beginning.'

Sebastian got down to the wharf just as the ferry was disappearing into the distance. His eyes blurred but not from staring at the shrinking vessel, nor was it because of the onshore breeze.

Behind him his bodyguards were pushing back against the assembled crowd, some of whom were holding placards with disgusting words and phrases written on them about Cassie.

Sebastian strode over and, ignoring the protests of his security team, faced the loud-mouthed crowd. He was aware of cameras flashing and every word he said being recorded, but he no longer cared. He tore strips off the gathering of people, telling them of the injustice Cassandra Kyriakis had suffered, not just at her father's hands all her young life, but at the hands of the courts who had wrongly imprisoned her just because she had tried to protect herself from her father's violence.

The crowd gradually began to disperse, like a pack of dogs that had been heavily chastened; their tails were between their legs as they slunk away.

Stefanos opened the car door for Sebastian. 'You do realise that will be all over the press tomorrow, Your Highness?'

Sebastian gave him an I-couldn't-care-less shrug. 'If it is I will not be here to read it,' he said with a set mouth.

'May I ask where you will be, Your Highness?'

Sebastian glanced at the palace and then back at the faint

outline of the ferry. 'I will give you one guess,' he said with a slowly spreading smile.

'Does that mean you will require the royal helicopter, Your Highness?'

Sebastian turned to look at his aide. 'You bet I will,' he said, still smiling. 'Take me to the heliport immediately.'

Once Cassie had settled Sam for a nap in the tiny villa she had chosen on the Greek Island of Ithaki, she came out to the terrace to breathe in the clean, salty air. The less populated island had appealed to her, for, although it didn't have a great choice of tourist-friendly beaches, the lack of tourists meant she and Sam could melt into the background until she decided where to finally go to rebuild her life.

The sound of footsteps behind her made her turn, her eyes going to the size of saucers when she saw Sebastian standing there.

'Are you out here to weave your shroud?' he asked.

Cassie frowned in bewilderment. 'Pardon?'

Amusement danced in his eyes. 'You don't know the legend of Penelope and Odysseus?'

'Yes…sort of…'

'The ancient island of Ithaca, now known as Ithaki, was Odysseus's long-lost home,' he explained. 'Legend has it Penelope sat waiting for him to return to her, weaving a shroud to keep her suitors at bay, for they believed he was dead, and she had told them once the shroud was finished she would choose one of them. But each night she cleverly un-ravelled her work while she waited for Odysseus to return.'

Cassie felt something move inside her chest. 'I wouldn't know the first thing about weaving….'

'Perhaps that is a good thing,' he said, 'for I would not want this particular suitor to be put off.'

She kept staring at him, trying to make sense of his words, hope like a tiny flickering flame inside her, struggling to warm the chill of the heartache she had suffered in leaving that morning.

'Aren't you going to say something?' he asked.

She pressed her lips together for a moment before she returned her eyes to his. 'If you've come to see Sam I'm afraid he's just settled down for a nap,' she said. 'He was a bit seasick on the way.'

'I would love to see Sam, but first I would like to talk to you.'

Cassie shifted her weight from foot to foot, her teeth having another go at her bottom lip. 'Look, if it's about the journalist I spoke to on the ferry across—'

'It's not about a journalist, and if you spoke to one then it can't have been any worse than what I said to the paparazzi and your send-off crowd down at the wharf,' he said with a wry twinkling smile. 'I am almost looking forward to seeing tomorrow's papers.'

She frowned at him. 'You spoke to the press?'

He gave her a tender look. 'Did you think I would not defend you, *agape mou?*'

Cassie didn't know what to think. She was struggling to contain her emotions, her heart was beating so hard and so fast her head felt as if it were spinning.

Sebastian came up to her and took her hands in his. 'Caz, I should have said this the day you told me about Sam—in fact I should have told you when you told me about your father and his treatment of you.'

She looked into his eyes. 'T-told me what?'

'You can't guess?'

She shook her head.

He brought her hands up to his mouth, pressing a soft kiss to each of her knuckles as he held her gaze. 'I love you,' he said. 'I have loved you for so long it felt like a limb was being torn off when you and Sam left. I was called back to the palace over some minor issue that was trumped up as being urgent because I suspect everyone knew I was going to stop you from leaving if I spent another minute with you.'

'We have no future, Seb,' she said. 'You know that. The throne is—'

'Empty until Alex makes up his mind whether he will take it or not,' he said. 'I do not want to rule unless you are by my side. You complete me, Caz, in a way no one else has or could ever do. This is not just about Sam—I need you to know that. If the people will not accept you as my wife then I will gladly relinquish the throne and all it entails.'

Cassie couldn't believe what she was hearing. She wanted to slap at her head, to make sure she hadn't imagined it. 'Your...*wife?*' she finally managed to croak. 'You want me to marry you?'

He smiled at her with love shining in his eyes. 'As soon as it can be arranged,' he said. 'We have been robbed of so much time. I want to make you my wife and start working on a brother or sister for Sam. We can be a family at last. It doesn't matter to me if it is on Aristo or somewhere else. But I suspect, after what I said to the press this morning, you will become the princess of the people in no time at all.'

Cassie couldn't hold back the tears; they dripped from her eyes as she hugged him close. 'I just want to be *your* princess,' she said.

He wrapped his arms around her, holding her tightly against him. 'You have always been my princess, Caz, the princess of my heart.'

There was the patter of little footsteps on the terrace, and a little voice squealed, 'Daddy! You've come to visit!'

Sebastian smiled as he scooped his little son up into his arms. 'Not just to visit, Sam,' he said, hugging him tightly. 'I am here to stay.'

* * * * *

We chatted to Melanie Milburne about the world of THE ROYAL HOUSE OF KAREDES. *Here are her insights!*

Would you prefer to live on Aristo or Calista?

I would definitely like to live on Aristo! All those beaches and majestic buildings such as the Karedes Palace and secluded hideaways.

What did you enjoy about writing about the Royal House of Karedes?

I really enjoyed getting to know the characters and seeing them develop as they realized their destiny, in particular Sebastian, who had so much pressure on his shoulders. Cassie was one of my favorite heroines as she was so courageous and her love for Sebastian had withstood almost impossible odds.

How did you find writing as part of a continuity?

It is always an amazing privilege to be part of a continuity knowing you are amongst brilliant authors and that you have been specially chosen to join them. It's quite daunting in fact!

When you are writing, what is your typical day?

I am quite a disciplined person (some would say obsessive!) so I like to get all my other tasks out of the way before I write. I swim first thing and then catch up on e-mails and do any shopping that needs to be done, plus take my dogs for a walk. I usually write all afternoon with lots of breaks for cups of tea and cookies.

Where do you get the inspiration for your characters?

I am a voracious reader and a people-watcher so I guess I would have to say a combination of life and reading, both fiction and nonfiction. Often it is just a phrase I have read that triggers a "what if" question in my head and then away I go.

What did you like most about your hero and heroine in this continuity?

I loved Cassie's spirit, which in spite of all she had suffered had not been broken. I loved Sebastian's self-sacrifice in that he was prepared to give up his right to the throne for the woman he loved.

What would be the best—and worst—things about being part of a royal dynasty?

I have a friend whose sister is a princess so I know how hard it is to have any real privacy. It would be so difficult to have hundreds of cameras thrust in your face all the time and not have any normalcy in your life. No ducking out for a coffee and shopping, for instance. But then a handsome prince more than makes up for it, right?

Are diamonds really a girl's best friend?

No, I think a loving partner who stands by you no matter what is a girl's best friend. Diamonds are definitely a bonus though!

Who will reunite the Stefani Diamond and rule Adamas?
Look for the next book in the fabulous
THE ROYAL HOUSE OF KAREDES:
RUTHLESS BOSS, ROYAL MISTRESS
by Natalie Anderson
Available January 2010

"THIS EVENING I'm flying to New York for two weeks," Jasim imparted with a casualness that made her vulnerable heart sink like a stone. "That's why I had you brought here. I own this apartment and you'll be comfortable here while I'm abroad."

"I can afford my own accommodation, although I may not need it for long. I'll have another job by the time you get back—"

Jasim released a slightly harsh laugh. "There's no need for you to look for another position. How would I ever see you? Don't you understand what I'm offering you?"

Elinor stood very still. "No. I must be incredibly thick because I haven't quite worked out yet what you're offering me...."

His charismatic smile slashed his lean dark visage. "Naturally, I want to take care of you...."

"No, thanks." Elinor forced a smile and mentally willed him not to demean her with some sordid proposition. "The only man who will ever take *care* of me with my agreement will be my husband. I'm willing to wait for you to come back, but I'm not willing to be kept by you. I'm a very independent woman and what I give, I give freely."

Jasim frowned. "You make it all sound so serious."

"What happened between us last night left pure chaos in

its wake," she reminded him gently. "Right now, I don't know whether I'm on my head or my heels. I'll stay for a while because I have nowhere else to go in the short term. So maybe it's good that you'll be away for a while."

Jasim pulled out his wallet to extract a card. "My private number," he told her, presenting her with it as though it was a precious gift—which indeed it was. Many women would have done just about anything to gain access to that direct hotline to him, but his staff guarded his privacy with scrupulous care.

Before he could close the wallet, his blood ran cold in his veins. How could he have made such a serious oversight? What if he had got her pregnant? He knew that an unplanned pregnancy would engulf his life like an avalanche, crush his freedom and suffocate him. He barely stilled a shudder at the threat of such an outcome, and thought how ironic it was that what his older brother had longed and prayed for—to secure the line to the throne—should strike Jasim as an absolute disaster....

* * * * *

Look out for two more enthralling stories in the
PREGNANT BRIDES *saga:*
RUTHLESS MAGNATE, CONVENIENT WIFE
is available in February
and GREEK TYCOON, INEXPERIENCED MISTRESS
in March.
Available wherever Harlequin books are sold.

HARLEQUIN *Presents*

TWO CROWNS, TWO ISLANDS, ONE LEGACY

A royal family torn apart by pride and its lust for power, reunited by purity and passion

Harlequin Presents is proud to bring you the final two installments from The Royal House of Karedes. As the stories unfold, secrets and sins from the past are revealed and desire, love and passion war with royal duty!

Look for:

RUTHLESS BOSS, ROYAL MISTRESS
by Natalie Anderson
January 2010

THE DESERT KING'S HOUSEKEEPER BRIDE
by Carol Marinelli
February 2010

HARLEQUIN *Presents*

Bestselling Harlequin Presents author

Lynne Graham

brings you an exciting new miniseries:

PREGNANT BRIDES

Inexperienced and expecting, they're forced to marry

Collect them all:

DESERT PRINCE, BRIDE OF INNOCENCE

January 2010

RUTHLESS MAGNATE, CONVENIENT WIFE

February 2010

GREEK TYCOON, INEXPERIENCED MISTRESS

March 2010

You've read the book, now see how the story began...in the hit game!

HARLEQUIN *Presents*

HIDDEN OBJECT OF DESIRE

*The first-ever Harlequin romance series game
for your PC or Mac™ computer*

The feud that fuels the passion in the Royal House of Karedes all began when an assassin set his eyes on the Prince of Aristo. Dive into the drama to find out how it all began in an amazing interactive game based on your favorite books!

Hidden Object of Desire is now available online at
www.bigfishgames.com/harlequin
Try the game for free!

Brought to you by Harlequin and Big Fish Games

HPBIGFISHR

REQUEST YOUR FREE BOOKS!

HARLEQUIN *Presents*

2 FREE NOVELS PLUS 2 FREE GIFTS!

PASSION GUARANTEED SEDUCTION

YES! Please send me 2 FREE Harlequin Presents® novels and my 2 FREE gifts (gifts are worth about $10). After receiving them, if I don't wish to receive any more books, I can return the shipping statement marked "cancel". If I don't cancel, I will receive 6 brand-new novels every month and be billed just $4.05 per book in the U.S. or $4.74 per book in Canada. That's a savings of close to 15% off the cover price! It's quite a bargain! Shipping and handling is just 50¢ per book*. I understand that accepting the 2 free books and gifts places me under no obligation to buy anything. I can always return a shipment and cancel at any time. Even if I never buy another book, the two free books and gifts are mine to keep forever.

106 HDN EYRQ 306 HDN EYR2

Name	(PLEASE PRINT)	
Address		Apt. #
City	State/Prov.	Zip/Postal Code

Signature (if under 18, a parent or guardian must sign)

Mail to the **Harlequin Reader Service**:
IN U.S.A.: P.O. Box 1867, Buffalo, NY 14240-1867
IN CANADA: P.O. Box 609, Fort Erie, Ontario L2A 5X3

Not valid to current subscribers of Harlequin Presents books.

Are you a current subscriber of Harlequin Presents books and want to receive the larger-print edition? Call 1-800-873-8635 today!

* Terms and prices subject to change without notice. Prices do not include applicable taxes. Sales tax applicable in N.Y. Canadian residents will be charged applicable provincial taxes and GST. Offer not valid in Quebec. This offer is limited to one order per household. All orders subject to approval. Credit or debit balances in a customer's account(s) may be offset by any other outstanding balance owed by or to the customer. Please allow 4 to 6 weeks for delivery. Offer available while quantities last.

Your Privacy: Harlequin Books is committed to protecting your privacy. Our Privacy Policy is available online at www.eHarlequin.com or upon request from the Reader Service. From time to time we make our lists of customers available to reputable third parties who may have a product or service of interest to you. If you would prefer we not share your name and address, please check here. ☐

HP09R

HARLEQUIN
Ambassadors

Want to share your passion for reading Harlequin® Books?

Become a Harlequin Ambassador!

Harlequin Ambassadors are a group of passionate and well-connected readers who are willing to share their joy of reading Harlequin® books with family and friends.

You'll be sent all the tools you need to spark great conversation, including free books!

All we ask is that you share the romance with your friends and family!

You'll also be invited to have a say in new book ideas and exchange opinions with women just like you!

To see if you qualify* to be a Harlequin Ambassador, please visit www.HarlequinAmbassadors.com.

Thank you for your participation.

BAP09BPA

I ♥ HARLEQUIN Presents

BROUGHT TO YOU BY FANS OF
HARLEQUIN PRESENTS.

We are its editors and authors
and biggest fans—and we'd
love to hear from YOU!

Subscribe today to our online blog at
www.iheartpresents.com